About This Book

What do you do when you've agreed to a pact with your friends to get married, but neither you nor the guy in your sights is quite ready to fall in love?

Bailey De Luca is the last of her friends to complete the Last First Date pact--to marry the next guy she dates. But lady luck must be in a bad mood because so far, it's all come to nothing.

Everywhere she looks people are in love. Everyone except her. Is she fundamentally unlovable? Or is it that she's already found--and lost--The One? Whatever the reason, one thing's for sure: Bailey never expected to be alone at thirty.

When one of her friends announces her engagement with a rock that could eclipse the sun, Bailey throws herself into a new business. Starting up Cozy Cottage Catering seems like the perfect way to bury her head in the sand. But fate has other ideas, and soon Bailey is swept off her feet by the oh-so cute Ryan Jones.

Ryan may seem like the perfect combination of Prince Charming meets Thor (without the hammer), but is Bailey ready to be with him?

Or will the ghost of her past love prevent her from finding happiness again?

FOUR LAST FIRST DATES

A romantic comedy of love, friendship...and one big cake

Cozy Cottage Café
Book 4

KATE O'KEEFFE

Wild Lime Books

Four Last First Dates is a work of fiction. The characters and events portrayed in this book are fictitious. Any similarity to real persons, living or dead, is purely coincidental and not intended by the author.

ISBN-13: 978-1721145317

Edited by Karan & Co. Author Solutions

Wild Lime

Books

Also by Kate O'Keeffe

It's Complicated Series:

Never Fall for Your Back-Up Guy

Never Fall for Your Enemy

Never Fall for Your Fake Fiancé

Never Fall for Your One that Got Away

Love Manor Romantic Comedy Series:

Dating Mr. Darcy

Marrying Mr. Darcy

Falling for Another Darcy

Falling for Mr. Bingley (spin-off novella)

High Tea Series:

No More Bad Dates

No More Terrible Dates

No More Horrible Dates

Cozy Cottage Café Series:

One Last First Date

Two Last First Dates

Three Last First Dates

Four Last First Dates

Wellywood Romantic Comedy Series:

Styling Wellywood

Miss Perfect Meets Her Match

Falling for Grace

Standalone title:

One Way Ticket

Writing as Lacey Sinclair:

Manhattan Cinderella

The Right Guy

Chapter 1

"TELL ME SOMETHING. DID IT HURT?" The guy I'd known for less than fifteen seconds leaned his hairless, muscular arms on the sticky wooden table, his blue eyes dancing.

I blinked, trying to understand his question. "Did *what* hurt, exactly?"

"You know, when you fell down to Earth from Heaven." Satisfied with his pick-up line, he sat back against the vinyl booth seat, flicked his 'seventies Bee Gees hair, and raised his eyebrows in expectation.

I did an internal eye roll. That had to be the tackiest line I'd heard tonight—and I was afraid to report, I'd heard a few. There was something about the short amount of time you got in speed dating that brought out the cheesy in these guys.

I was beginning to regret ever having agreed to this.

I forced a smile. "Oh, sure. I get it. I'm an angel who fell to Earth. That's a good one." I tried not to allow the sleaze-factor crawl across my skin.

Oh, how I wished this whole thing could be over and I could go home, throw on Netflix, and eat leftover cake from the Cozy

Cottage Café. *So* much better than having to listen to guys like this one try to "charm me."

"Shame I wasn't there to catch you. I'm very strong, you know." He flexed his bulging muscles, just to make sure I got the message.

"I bet."

Satisfied with my response, he flashed me a row of perfect pearly whites as he stroked his chin. His thick, designer five-o'clock shadow must have felt like sandpaper.

I glanced over at my friends sitting at the bar—Cassie, Paige, and Marissa—working hard at pretending not to watch my every move. I gotta tell you, they weren't doing a good job. As soon as they noticed me glaring at them, all three of them snapped their heads away, focusing on anything but me.

Thanks a lot, girls.

Still, I could only blame myself for the predicament I found myself in, sitting across from this guy, listening to his dreadful pick-up lines. You see, I was at this speed dating event down at O'Dowd's Pub because I was trying to find my Last First Date.

Yes, that's right. I was trying to find the last man I'd ever go out with. The man I would marry. Although right now, I'd have preferred to forget the whole darn thing.

Why was I subjecting myself to this torture, you may ask? It's a good question, and one that had me glancing at the exit with longing in my eyes.

It's a long story. Suffice it to say, I'd agreed to a pact with those three friends of mine at the bar to marry the next guy I dated—just like they had.

Totally insane, right? Certifiable, even. Well, *optimistic* at the very least.

But whatever a shrink might have to say about it, it meant I needed to find Mr. Right, which was what I was trying to do tonight. And he had to be Mr. Right—not Mr. Okay, Mr. He'll Do, or even Mr. Right For Now.

No way.

I wasn't settling for anything less than the absolute perfect guy for me. Because I'd already been there with the guy I thought *was* perfect for me, the one I planned on spending my life with.

Yet here I sat, single, alone, still looking for love.

The good news was that the pact had worked for Cassie, Paige, and Marissa. All three of them were happily and blissfully in love with their respective guys.

Now, it was my turn. Although looking at the Bee Gees wannabe across the table from me, I was having *serious* second thoughts about the whole darn thing.

I clenched my fists under the table, determined to turn this conversation around. I decided to change it to something less . . . *icky*.

I cleared my throat. "You sound British. Are you?"

"I am. London, born and bred," he replied, tilting his chin up and puffing out his chest. His accent definitely sounded cockney, more like Michael Cain than Hugh Grant.

"I love London. What do you do, ah—" I glanced down at the name tag clipped to his white open-necked shirt, "—Jamie?"

He leant back in. "Actually, I'm going to let you in on a little secret, darlin'."

I pressed my lips together. If his opening line was anything to go by, I wasn't so sure I wanted to hear one of his "little secrets."

"Jamie's not my real name."

"Oh?" I wondered why he chose not to have his actual name on a name tag at a speed dating event.

He shook his head. "He's my idol, you see. Jamie Oliver."

That piqued my interest. "Really? I adore Jamie Oliver!"

He shrugged. "A lot of people do. I'm a chef. Pretty famous where I'm from, actually." He shot me a self-satisfied look.

"Famous, huh?"

What was he doing speed dating at O'Dowd's Pub in downtown Auckland, literally on the other side of the world, if he was famous?

"Yeah, it's a bit of a drag. I used to get fans throwing themselves at me. Female fans, usually, of course." He raised his eyebrows, as if to say "see how desirable I am?"

I didn't.

Instead, I had an image of a group of frenzied women lunging themselves at him, a frightened look on his face as he scrambled to get away. I had to stifle a giggle.

"That's why I'm here, you see. I want to meet someone real, someone who doesn't know me or my work. Know what I mean?"

"Well, I don't know you or your work, *Jamie.*"

"Exactly." His eyes dropped to my chest and lingered there. I self-consciously pulled at my top.

I glanced down at the checklist of questions I'd prepared for tonight. With only four minutes per "date," I'd decided I wanted to make the conversation as targeted as possible—without making the guys feel like they were being interrogated by the S.S.

Well, maybe a little interrogated. This *was* meant to be my Last First Date, after all.

I looked back up at Fake Jamie—although with the flicked hair and square jaw he looked much more like a Fabio-wannabe than the chef. "So, tell me, with the limited time we have right now, what do you want me to know about you?"

Clearly not your name . . .

I'd gotten that question from a list on the Internet. I liked it because it wasn't your usual "what do you do for a living" and "where are you from" line of questioning. And it would hopefully tell me something a little more interesting about each of these men I was meeting tonight.

I sat back and waited for the cheese to ooze right out of him.

I wasn't disappointed.

"Only that you're the most beautiful woman in this room, and if you don't let me take you home tonight, I think I may die." His eyes slid down to my chest once more where they remained for some time.

Really, I could've vomited.

I smiled weakly at him. Four minutes with this guy suddenly felt like a *lifetime.*

He reached across the table and placed his hand on top of mine.

It was warm and clammy. In the interests of being polite, I resisted the urge to pull away—and apply a serious amount of hand sanitizer.

"Bailey. That's such a beautiful name."

"Thank you." I slipped my hand out from under his, shooting him a smile.

"Are you named after the milky liqueur?"

The liqueur? Was he *crazy*? Who named their child after an alcoholic drink?

"Ah, no. It's a family name. From my dad's side."

"So, our firstborn daughter could be 'Bailey,' too."

Our *what*? Man, this guy was laying it on by the shovel load.

I laughed nervously, my eyes darting over to my friends once more. Cassie gave me a hopeful look, her hesitant "thumbs up" gesture completely at odds with the way I felt about Fake Jamie—his blatant advances *and* Fabio looks.

Not that I had anything against this Fabio slash Fake Jamie guy, of course, but I didn't think I wanted to date him. Let alone have children with him.

My eyes drifted from Cassie to a tall, imposing man standing beside Marissa. After a moment, I recognized him, my tummy doing an involuntary flip as my eyes glided over him. Ryan Jones, Marissa's older brother. He didn't look like he did when I last saw him. Sure, he was just as tall, broad, and athletic looking, just as cute—not that I'd noticed any of that before of course.

Oh, okay, I *had* noticed. In my defense, it was hard not to notice a guy like Ryan. Tall, wide shouldered, handsome, charming. You got the picture.

He was dressed in a pair of jeans and a shirt with the sleeves rolled up, exposing his strong arms. *That* hadn't changed. But now, his dirty blonde hair was longer than before, sexier, like he'd just messed it up absent-mindedly with his fingers. He was also sporting a new close-cut beard. And it suited him.

I bit my lip.

Put a hammer in his hand and he'd look like freaking Thor.

The last time I'd seen Ryan Jones was the night Marissa had performed a song for her Last First Date, Nash, at my café. Ryan had flirted with me and made me smile. I didn't think much of it at the time. You see, he'd flirted with me once before and nothing had come of it. I figured it didn't mean anything.

Although I'd wished it had.

His eyes found mine, and he flashed his handsome grin. I smiled back before tearing my eyes back to my "date."

"Umm, I'm not sure we should get that far ahead of ourselves. You know, selecting names for our first born," I said.

There would be no firstborns called Bailey—or anything else with this guy for that matter. And I could tell you one thing right now; there wouldn't even be a second date.

Mercifully, the bell rang, indicating our speed date had come to an end.

I smiled at him across the table. "Nice to meet you Fa-Jamie." I pressed my lips together, glad I caught the nickname I'd given him in my head before it completely escaped my lips.

"You too, beautiful Bailey." He reached across the table for my hand, but there was no way I was letting his clammy mitts get ahold of me again. Instead, his hand made contact with my elbow which, rather weirdly, he didn't let go of.

Awkward much?

"I'll be back later to take you home." His gaze was intense.

I let out a small shudder.

Before I could say "vomit bag," another guy materialized at my table. He shot us a puzzled look, and I couldn't blame him. You didn't see a man awkwardly holding a woman's elbow over a table every day of the week.

"Ah, I think you're needed at the next one, mate," New Guy said, nodding at the table beside mine where a petite blonde woman with a top that plunged almost to her navel was seated.

Fake Jamie glanced over at the woman, who smiled back at him. In a flash, he dropped my elbow and sauntered over to her table, flicking his Bee Gees hair as he went.

I let out a relieved puff of air and glanced at the woman, hoping she could manage him better than I had.

New Guy sat down in the now-vacant spot, and the whole thing started over again.

"Hey, I'm Adam." He reached across and we shook hands. "And you're—" He glanced at my nametag then back up into my eyes. "Bailey."

Already, things were off to a better start than the previous four minutes of my life. Which, let's face it, wasn't exactly hard.

"Hi, Adam. It's great to meet you." I flashed a smile, more than a little relieved this guy seemed normal—so far, anyway.

And did I mention quite cute, too?

"So, shall we begin? I mean we only have four minutes," Adam said.

"Exactly."

"Right. Bailey, what's the one thing about yourself you would like me to know?"

I let out a laugh. "That's my question!"

"Really?" His smile was broad, and I noticed how open and kind his face was. He wasn't Hollywood-star handsome, with his slightly receding hairline and eyebrows a beauty therapist would have a field day with, but he seemed nice—and a million miles from Fake Jamie's creepiness.

"I just asked that last guy the very same question. His answer was . . . how do I put this?"

"Too smooth?" Adam replied.

Adam and I both glanced over at the adjacent couple where Fake Jamie was leaning across the table and had taken the petite blonde woman's hands in his. I guessed he was delivering the same lines as he had to me. She looked about as enthralled as I had been.

Poor girl.

Adam returned his attention to me. "I should be honest with you. I did some research online to find questions for this speed dating thing. You see, I've not done it before, and my friends kind of pushed me into it."

I glanced across at my own friends, sipping their wine and being about as subtle as a sledgehammer as they watched me and Adam on our "date."

"You know what? I can relate to that."

"You got railroaded into this, too, huh?"

I shrugged. "Kind of. It was my friend Marissa's suggestion, but I guess I'm the one sitting here, right?"

"Right." He smiled, and I couldn't help but return it.

This is going well. Maybe Marissa was right? Maybe "going old school" by speed dating instead of using those dating apps or sites was the right thing to do?

"Anyway, to answer your question, I guess I would like you to know that I'm here genuinely looking for someone."

His smile grew. "That's good to know. Me too. Or, at least, I am now."

Unlike with Fake Jamie, the compliment didn't have even a whiff of cheese to it. In fact, it was . . . nice.

"Ready for my next question? I've got a huge list." He laughed.

"Sure. Fire away."

"What are you most proud of?"

"Great question! I hadn't seen that one."

"Thanks. It's all in a day's work."

"Okay, I guess it would have to be my business."

"What do you do?"

"I run a café, and I love it." I thought of the Cozy Cottage Café and smiled. I'd been running it with Paige, my dear, sweet friend, for some time now, and we had taken it to new heights. We were always busy, feeding and watering the masses in our homely, welcoming café.

"A café? Nice. I like coffee. And eating."

I laughed. "Well, you should stop by some time."

"What's it called?"

I told him about the Cozy Cottage, and we continued to chat, the four minutes whizzing by. All too soon, the bell sounded, and Adam got up to leave.

"I hope to see you again." The skin around his eyes crinkled as a smile lit up his face.

"You, too."

I looked over at the girls, all three giving me the thumbs up. I beamed at them.

Perhaps this speed dating thing hadn't been such a bad idea, after all?

Chapter 2

THE NEXT GUY WAS so nondescript and dull, not even my list of probing and unusual questions helped. And I wasn't here for nondescript and dull. I was here to find "The One."

Well, that was the plan at least.

As I sat half listening to Nondescript Guy carry on about how important his health was and how he liked to have granola each morning to keep himself "regular"—talking about bowel movements on a date? Really?—I did my best to stifle a yawn.

I scanned the room. I could see Fake Jamie-slash-Fabio chatting up some new victim, and Adam talking with Perky Blonde at the adjacent table. Marissa waved at me from the bar, catching my eye. She shrugged, her palms face up as she nodded at my current "date."

I gave my head one shake to indicate Nondescript Guy was a non-starter, and she scrunched her face up.

I stole another glance at Ryan. He and Paige were deep in conversation, and he didn't look my way.

". . . and you see, that's why the flora of your gut is so important," Nondescript Guy said, an earnest look on his face. "Not a lot of people know that, but it's vital for good health."

"Absolutely," I replied, having no clue what he was talking about. Wasn't flora a word scientists used for plants? I thought remembered it vaguely from high school biology.

"I'm glad you understand. That's important to me, to have a partner on the same health journey as me."

I blinked, unsure how to respond. A "health journey" didn't exactly sound like something I could get on board with. You see, I had a bit of a cake habit. Baking, eating, the lot. And I had a great excuse—my café was known for its cakes. We always had a variety to suit most tastes, even offering a couple of gluten-free options lately, too.

Although I'm not sure Nondescript Guy and his "health journey" would approve of even those.

Fortunately, the bell sounded, so I didn't have to pass comment. Instead, I smiled and said, "Nice to meet you."

He got up and moved on to Perky Blonde. I heaved a sigh of relief.

"Hello."

I looked up to see a small, bespectacled man standing by my table. He was dressed in a button-down shirt and khaki pants. He looked more than a little nervous.

"Hi," I said brightly, trying to put him at ease. Although he didn't look like they type of guy I'd dated in the past, I knew I needed to keep an open mind. "Please, take a seat."

"Oh, I err . . . okay." He pulled a pad and pencil out from his back pocket and sat down opposite me.

I glanced at his name tag. "Your name is Reg? Is that short for Reginald?"

He nodded. "Lieutenant Reginald Barclay the third, actually."

Lieutenant? Very formal. He didn't look much like a military man, with his slim frame and lack of stature. But who was I to judge?

"Nice," I said with a smile, trying not to let on what I was thinking.

"It's not 'nice.'" He scowled at me as though I'd insulted him.

"Lieutenant Reginald Barclay is the most underrated member of the Starship Enterprise."

The what now?

"Oh." Not for the first time tonight, I didn't know quite what to say.

"It's all Captain Kirk and Spock, the superstars of the series."

"This is a *Star Wars* thing?"

"*Star Wars*?" he spat, his features forming a disapproving scowl.

You'd think I'd insulted his mother.

"*Star* Trek." He shook his head, his lips forming a thin line. "Reginald is a crew member of the Starship Enterprise."

"Gotcha." I didn't at all.

"He needs his time in the spotlight, too, you know. He was a technical genius, not one of those 'look at me, I'm an alpha male' types." He glared at me as though I was personally responsible for this Reginald Whatshisname's lack of superstar status. "Beta males are just as important for the procreation of the species."

I cleared my throat. *Is this guy for real?*

I glanced down at his notepad, landing on a way to move the conversation on. "You've come prepared."

"Yes, I . . . have some key questions I'm looking for answers to."

"Okay," I replied, steeling myself for what was to come.

He flipped the notepad open and studied his notes.

I waited and waited.

And waited.

I shot my friends a desperate look I hoped they could read. It went something like "get me the heck out of here!"

"Ah, excuse me, Reg?"

He looked up at me as though I were some sort of irritation to him. "What?"

"We only have four minutes together. You know that, right?"

"Yes, yes." He waved his hand in the air at me.

I knitted my eyebrows together. This was feeling less like a date and more like a visit to the school principal.

"Aha!" he exclaimed, making me jump.

"You've found your question?"

"Yes, I have."

"Great."

"What is your bust measurement?"

My mouth dropped open. "My *bust* measurement?"

"Yes." His tone was matter-of-fact tone. "Your bust measurement, otherwise known as the circumference of your . . .err chestal area." He made a circular motion in the air with his hands.

I crossed my arms on the table in front of my "bust." I cleared my throat. "Why do you want to know *that*?"

"Because I assessed you as you arrived, and you have the proportions I am most invested in."

What? Invested? Proportions? What was this guy, a freaking mad scientist? Or, worse yet, a serial killer?

"Invested in for a date?" I asked, really not wanting to know the answer.

"Of course!" he replied a little too loudly. "Why else would I be here? There isn't any other explanation. I'm here for the dating. I want to meet someone to date."

I wasn't buying it. I glanced down at his notepad. There were numbers scrawled over the page. I let out a laugh, hoping to lighten the mood. "I don't know. Maybe you're doing some research or something?"

He pursed his lips and glared at me. "Who said that?" His eyes darted around the room in accusation.

I shifted in my seat. "Ah, me?"

He let out a puff of air. "I'm here for the dating, and as part of that, I would like to know what your bust measurements is, thank you."

To my astonishment, he half-stood and reached into his front pocket, pulling a blue plastic measuring tape out in a long coil.

"You're serious?" I guffawed. I shot a nervous look over at my friends. They all had incredulous looks on their faces, watching the bizarre speed date with "Reg"—allegedly the most underrated of the Starship Enterprise crew—unfold before their eyes.

"I thought I'd made that clear already. Do you have an objection?"

I crossed my arms. "Actually, I do."

His glasses slid down his nose, and he pushed them back up his face with his index finger. "Well, in that case, I will need to hug you."

"Hug me?"

This was getting more and more perverse.

"Yes. That way I can assess you, since my measuring tape appears to be so abhorrent to you." His tone suggested I was slow on the uptake and he needed to explain things more clearly. "It won't be as accurate, of course, but if you won't provide me with your consent, I shall have no choice."

That was it. I'd had enough. I placed my hands palm-down on the table. "Look, Reg—or whatever your actual name is. I'm not interested in being assessed or measured or anything. So, can you please refrain from asking me again?"

He slumped in his chair. "But you're the best one."

"The best one for what?"

Why oh why did I have to ask?

He let out a puff of air. "I'm designing something, even if *Father* thinks it's a 'waste of my education.'" He did air quotes, his face contorted in bitterness.

"What are you designing?"

My mouth was clearly disconnected from my brain at this point.

"The perfect woman, only robotic so she won't have any of the challenges of a real woman."

Oh, no.

"She's going to be incredible. Beautiful, loving, flexible, do whatever you want . . ."

I held my hands up. "Stop!" I'd heard more than enough. I slid out of my chair and stood up.

Reginald Barclay III looked up at me in surprise. As I stepped around the table, he also stood and attempted to swing his measuring tape around me.

I grabbed a hold of one end of it and snapped it away from him. "You have *got* to be kidding me." I smacked the tape down on the table, turned and walked away, just as the bell sounded for the next round of "dates."

But there would be no more "dates" for me. I'd had more than enough Jamie wannabes and sicko mad scientist guys to last me a lifetime.

I was done.

Chapter 3

"HE WANTED TO *MEASURE* you?" Cassie's face a study in disbelief.

I nodded, my arms crossed. Like Queen Victoria, I was *so* not amused.

"Bailey, I'm sorry," Paige said, her hand on my arm. "I had no idea there'd be such crazies at these things."

"Crazy" was definitely a massive understatement for Reginald Barclay III. The guy was making a sex robot, for goodness' sake. And he wanted to base its bust measurement on *me*!

I shuddered at the thought.

"It's not over, yet. Did you want to give it another try?" Marissa asked. "There are some normal looking guys here. Well, normal-ish."

I shot her a withering look. "Seriously?"

"I'll take that as a 'no,' then." Marissa shrunk back from me.

"Sorry, I'm just a little tightly wound."

"We get it," Cassie replied. "Don't we, Marissa?"

Marissa gave a reluctant nod. As I said, speed dating had been her idea. I guess she was more invested in the outcome than the others, especially as I was the last in the pact to find her man.

"I think four dates in one evening is more than enough, especially with the selection here," I added.

The four of us were standing in the ladies' room of O'Dowd's, the speed dating carrying on in the bar without me. Some poor schmuck was waiting at my empty table for a "date" I wouldn't be returning to any time soon.

"What about that second guy? He was cute. You liked him, right?" Paige was ever the optimist, looking for the silver lining to my speed dating disaster cloud.

I nodded. "Adam." He'd seemed nice and didn't appear to be a member of the nut bar squad. I shrugged. "I don't know. I guess I'm a bit put off by the whole thing right now."

"Give me your card." Marissa stretched her hand out and waited.

With a resigned sigh, I reached into my purse and pulled out my speed dating card. It had a list of the ten men here tonight. Ten? Wow, I'd only got through four before I'd had to escape. Six more Fake Jamies or Reginald Barclays would probably have killed me.

But according to the rules of our Last First Date pact, one of those men out there was supposed to be my HEA—my happily ever after. And you know what? Speed dating *had* seemed like a good idea; a smorgasbord of guys to choose from, all in one evening.

Low effort: high yield.

And I'd liked the odds—that was, until I'd met the guys. "Odd" didn't even begin to describe them.

I let out a sigh. I guess that meant I'd just been on a total of four Last First Dates, for a total of sixteen unpleasant minutes. Well, other than the four with Adam.

I handed the card to Marissa who clicked her pen. "Right, which was the crazy robot guy?"

"Reg Barclay."

She put a big cross next to his name. "And what about the guy with the long, flicky hair who looked like he was more than a little in love with himself?"

"He called himself 'Jamie.'"

"Strike him off." Marissa placed a large cross next to his name.

I smiled. There was actually something quite satisfying about doing this.

"Who was the guy you liked? Was it Adam?"

"That's him," Cassie confirmed.

"Tick?" Marissa looked at me, brows raised and pen poised.

I pulled a face. He seemed nice enough, and he was cute, but I just didn't know anymore.

Man, this dating thing was hard! No wonder I'd avoided it for so long since . . . well, since the last time.

"Come on, Bailey. What have you go to lose?" Paige encouraged.

I looked at my friends' hopeful faces. They were all watching me, waiting for my response.

I wanted what they had—a partner, someone to spend my life with. Someone to love. I needed to take this leap of faith.

Despite my reservations, I nodded, pressing my lips together.

Paige clapped her hands like an excited seal as Marissa drew a big tick next to Adam's name.

"Right, all you have to do now is turn this in to the convener and see whether Adam picked you," Marissa said as she handed me the card.

"Of course he would have picked Bailey. Look at her!" Cassie gestured at me.

"I know, right?" Paige said.

They all nodded like three bobblehead puppies in the back of a car.

I felt a blush bloom in my cheeks. "You guys."

It was sweet of them to compliment me, but if I had my way, I'd be several inches taller, shave a good few inches off my hips and thighs, and be able to go braless once in a while without being able to store a handful of pencils under there.

But then, I did love my food, and hell would freeze over before I gave that up. I thought of the guy on his "health journey." Did my love of food put me on a "cake journey?" I sure hoped so. I smiled at the thought.

We hung around in the ladies' room, waiting for the event to finish. Once we heard the convener announcing it was time to turn in our cards, we exited *en force*. I avoided eye contact with every man in the room as I made a B-line for the convener's table, my card held tightly in my hand.

"Thank you," he said, smiling up at me. "You'll find out if you have a match shortly."

I thanked him and returned to the sanctity of my friends, extremely relieved my inaugural speed dating session was now done and dusted. Inaugural and *last*, that was. Female robot designers and sleazy chefs had completely put me off trying anything like this ever again.

"Here, you may need this." Cassie handed me a glass of chilled white wine. I thanked her and immediately took a large glug.

"So, have you found the man of your dreams here tonight?" a deep voice said behind me.

I turned to see who it was, hoping—praying—it wasn't Fake Jamie, here to deliver a new sleazy line while looking down my top.

To my relief, it wasn't. I looked up into a pair of hazel eyes set into a handsome face, regarding me with gentle teasing.

Ryan Jones.

"Maybe?" I said with a smile, my tummy doing a flip at the sight of him.

He raised his eyebrows in response. "Did he have a good pick-up line? I've got some, you know."

"You do? Like what?"

He licked his lips, readying himself. "Okay, here's my best one. I hope you know C.P.R., because you just took my breath away."

I cocked an eyebrow. "Seriously?"

His lips curved into an easy smile. "What, you wouldn't fall for that one?"

I shook my head, laughing. "Um, that would be a 'no.'"

"Okay, how about this one. Were you in the Scouts? Because you sure have tied my heart into a knot."

A laugh escaped my lips. "That's actually not bad, for a totally cheesy line, that is."

"Thanks."

"Okay, I think I've got one."

"It had better be good."

"Oh, it is. Your name must be Google, because you have everything I'm searching for."

He nodded, grinning. "Not bad, De Luca, not bad."

I beamed. "Why thank you."

"I've got another."

"How could you possibly top my Google line?"

"It was good, but not that good. Take this one for a test drive. Do you believe in love at first sight, or should I walk past you again?"

I put my hand over my heart as I laughed once more, genuinely enjoying myself for the first time tonight. "Tell me you've never used one of those."

He shook his head, his gorgeous hazel eyes dancing. "No way."

"I'm glad to hear it. What are you doing here, anyway? Been doing the speed dating thing, too?"

"Me? Oh, no." He shook his head. "I'm just here for the beer. A much better idea."

I broadened my smile. "Good call." I raised my glass of wine, and he clinked his beer bottle against it. "Cheers."

"Cheers. Here's to *not* finding The One."

"Who said I haven't? He might be in this room right now."

"Yeah? Maybe he's that short guy over there, watching you closely. I think he's taking notes in his little pad."

Startled, I followed Ryan's line of sight to see Reg, intermittently studying me, his pencil doing overtime on his notepad.

"Oh, no." I maneuvered myself so Ryan's body obscured Reg's line of vision of me, hoping it would end his little note taking.

"Why is he doing that?" Ryan asked.

I let out a heavy sigh. "He's building a robot."

He raised his eyebrows, clearly amused. "He is? What type of . . .?" He looked over at Reg, who had moved himself to get a better view of me. "Oh, I get it. A *female* robot, right?"

I nodded, shifting closer to Ryan.

"And he wants to base her on you?"

"Yup."

He moved so he was once again in Reg's line of site. "Well, I can totally see why." Ryan's eyes slid back to me. "If I were a weird scientist guy making a pervy robot, I'd base it on you, too." A smile teased at the edges of his mouth.

My tummy did a massive flip in response. I had to resist the urge to giggle at the fact that a guy who looked a lot like Thor was currently shielding me from a mad scientist in a crowded bar—*and* he thought I was attractive.

Really, I couldn't make this stuff up.

"Err, thanks," I muttered, heat blooming in my cheeks.

"Want me to have a word?" He nodded at Reg, who had now wormed his way closer, his notepad and pencil still clutched in his hands.

As appealing as it was to have a Norse god defend my honor, I knew I could fight my own battles.

"No, but thanks anyway. Can you hold this for me?" I handed him my glass of wine.

"Sure."

I stepped out from behind Ryan and made my way past a group of people to Reg. Although I'm only a diminutive five foot four in my heels, I towered over him.

He looked up, what appeared to be a mixture of awe and fear in his eyes.

"Are you still taking notes?" I crossed my arms, glaring at him. My voice was calm, measured. I may still have been blushing from Ryan's compliment, but I wasn't the type to take this kind of treatment lying down.

He flipped the cover of his notepad over and clutched it against his puny body, his eyes darting around the room. "It's just research."

Before I had the chance to say another word, he ducked around me and zig-zagged through the crowd. I watched, open-mouthed, as he disappeared from sight, obscured by the regular-sized people in the bar.

Well, that was beyond weird.

I returned to Ryan and my glass of wine.

"What did you say to him to make him take off like that?" Ryan asked, shaking his head.

"Nothing much. I just asked him if he was still taking notes on me."

"Well, you had him running scared, that's for sure."

"Yeah, right back to his secret lab." I let out a laugh.

There was a loud screeching sound as the convener switched on his microphone. "Sorry about that, everyone. Feedback. Right, we have all the cards back and have made some matches!"

The crowd cheered, and I swallowed the nervous frog in my throat.

Had Adam chosen me?

Did I even *want* him to?

I glanced at Ryan. Of all the men in the room, he was easily the most interesting. And definitely hottest.

And the only one *not* here for the speed dating.

Just my luck.

"I'm happy to say we've had a record number of matches tonight. You guys are awesome!"

More cheering.

"Come on up and see me or Veronica, my lovely assistant over here." He gestured at a small, plump woman in her early twenties, who gave an embarrassed wave. "We will tell you who your love match is. You get to decide whether you want to give that person your contact details. And then, boys and girls, the rest is up to you. Only, if there are any weddings from tonight's matches, we do need to invite us."

There was a ripple of laughter around the pub.

"Do you think mad scientist guy chose you?" Ryan said into my ear. I tried to ignore the way his warm breath tingled my neck.

"He ran off, remember?"

"Oh, yeah. Pity. I could totally see you with him."

I shot him a quizzical look. "And you only get matched when both people choose each other, and I can assure you I did not chose him."

"Are you telling me you didn't want to date that guy?" Ryan was teasing, his eyes wide. "As long as I live, I will never understand women."

I slapped him playfully on the arm.

"Are you going to see if Adam chose you, too?" Marissa asked, materializing at my side then shooting Ryan a look.

"Who's Adam?" Ryan asked, his brows raised.

"Well, he could be Bailey's Last First Date," Marissa replied.

"You're in on that dating pact, too?" The expression on Ryan's face made it clear he didn't approve.

Of course, I knew the pact to marry the next guy I dated was a little juvenile, but I'd agreed to it. On a windswept beach around a bonfire, no less. Sure, there may have been a glass or two of wine involved, and maybe we did get swept up in the moment. But like the others, I wanted to find him, I wanted to find someone to share my life with.

I needed to own this.

"Yes, actually, Ryan. I am in on that dating pact." My eyes challenged him to respond.

He studied my face, his own eyes narrowed. I wanted to squirm. "Well, good luck then." He broke eye contact and took a swig of his beer.

"She doesn't need luck. It's fate, big brother. Just like it was for all of us," Marissa sniffed. She took me by the hand and lead me through the crowd to the convener's table.

I glanced back at Ryan. He had an impassive look on his face as he watched for a second before looking away once more, taking a fresh swig of his beer.

Marissa and I stood in line, waiting to find out if I would be chosen by the only guy I had on my list—or if I'd be humiliated.

"Don't go getting any ideas about my brother, okay?" Marissa said.

I swallowed, discomfited she had noticed Ryan and I flirting. Because that's definitely what it was—flirting. We did it whenever we saw one another. It never led anywhere, but it was fun all the same.

"He's still getting over Amelia, his ex. You know, she hurt him real bad."

I nodded. Amelia had dumped Ryan on his sorry butt and then moved onto the next guy fast enough to give her whiplash. When I first met Ryan, he was bitter and angry—despite being very cute.

"Of course. I know about it. He's not here to look for a date, anyway, so it's a moot point."

"Good. He's a great guy, but broken, totally broken."

Eventually, we reached Veronica, who handed me a card. "I'm sorry. No match for you tonight."

I knitted my brows together, examining the card closely as though she could have gotten it wrong.

Adam didn't pick me?

"Do you think you could check again, please? I'm sure this must have been some kind of mistake," Marissa said to Veronica, tapping her index finger on the table.

"No mistake," Veronica replied cheerily. "But we're here every week. Better luck next time."

I blinked at her upturned, shining face. The idea of coming back here and doing this all again was about as appealing as being slapped in the face by a large, wet fish.

"Err, thanks," I muttered as I turned to leave. Mortification crept up my legs and into my belly.

Adam didn't pick me.

"You know what? He was probably intimidated by you, that's all. You're good looking, successful, really sweet." Marissa slung her arm around my shoulders.

"Yeah, because guys hate women like that." I tried to keep the sour tone from my voice.

Yup, I failed.

"Oh, honey. We'll work something out, don't you worry." Marissa gave me a squeeze.

Paige came up behind us and slung her arms around our shoulders. "How many dates did you get, Bailey?"

Marissa glared at her as I replied, "None."

"What?" Paige's voice was ear-piercingly loud, even in the noisy pub. "How can that be? I mean, look at you."

I smiled weakly at her.

"There must be some kind of mix up. I know what. Why don't you go over and talk to him? I can see him over there, standing near Ryan." Paige nodded at the other side of the bar.

I looked over to see Adam talking with a man, nodding along to what he was saying. His back was to Ryan's, and I noticed they were both about the same height. I couldn't help but compare the two men. Ryan was easily the more imposing, better looking of the two, right down to his newly acquired Thor beard.

Strictly speaking, beards weren't really my thing. On Ryan, it looked good. *He* looked good.

Kissable, even.

Wait, *what?* I wanted to kiss Ryan?

Ryan, Marissa's older brother, the guy who had not that long ago had his heart ripped from his chest and trampled on by his ex?

A guy who made bitter chocolate taste sweet?

I shook my head, dislodging the thought. Sure, we'd flirted a bit, and it was fun, but that was as far as it was likely to go with Ryan and the complicated state of his heart.

Adam looked over in my direction and smiled. I immediately looked away, the sting of his rejection hitting me.

"No, no. I don't think I'll go talk to Adam," I said to Paige.

"Are you sure? I mean, tonight is meant to be your Last First Date. Don't you want to give it a final shot? The man of your dreams could be in this room."

I bit my lip as my eyes wandered back to the two men. Only, I wasn't looking at the guy who was meant to be my date.

I was looking at Ryan—his complicated heart and all.

Chapter 4

THE FOLLOWING MORNING, MY humiliation at not being picked by Adam reduced to a low, annoyed grumble, Paige and I busied ourselves with the comings and goings of the Cozy Cottage Café.

I had successfully pushed the unexpected romantic stirrings Ryan elicited in me firmly to the back of my mind. I wasn't about to go falling for him, despite the fact he was super fun to be around. He was easy-going, flirty, smart. And then there was the small fact he looked like a Norse god.

I let out a sigh. It was never a good idea to date your friend's brother. Too complicated. Especially if it doesn't work out.

And anyway, he only broke up with someone a matter of six months ago.

There was no way I was going there.

"I've finished that fresh batch of cream cheese frosting for the carrot cake," I said.

Paige's back was turned to me as she pulled a cake out of the oven with her mitts. "Thanks, Bailey." She placed the steaming cake on a rack on the counter. "I know we bake these cakes all the time, but I don't think I'll ever get tired of that delicious aroma."

Although I'd been running the café for some time now, Paige had joined me as my partner with an equal share in the business after she ditched a marketing career she hated. And I was very glad to have her on board. We made an excellent team, and the café ran like clockwork, both of us passionate about what we did.

We'd made a few changes to the place, such as introducing the wildly successful "Cozy Cottage Jam" music sessions on a Friday night, without losing any of the special character that made our café unique.

You see, even though the Cozy Cottage was situated in the hustle and bustle of downtown Auckland, my vision for it was as a relaxed and welcoming country cottage café. I wanted people to feel instantly at home the moment they walked through our front door, to sit and relax over a cup of Ned's Coffee, perhaps indulge in one of the many sweet treats we had on offer.

At first, I'd considered calling the place "Stop and Smell the Roses," because that's what I wanted people to do. I ended up with "Cozy Cottage" after I'd stumbled across my idea of a perfect country café in Devon on a trip to England. I'd fallen in love with the homely charm of the place, and once back home in New Zealand, I set about finding the perfect spot to replicate it.

The Cozy Cottage Café had been my passion, my happy place, ever since.

"Morning, chicks!" Sophie's bright voice called out as she bustled by me on her way to the back of the kitchen. "Sorry I'm late. The traffic is mad out there today."

"No worries, Sophie."

Sophie joined the staff when I'd first opened the café doors about eighteen months ago, and she was my most reliable barista—traffic issues this morning aside. It helped that she was incredibly sweet, too.

I picked up a *Cassata alla Siciliana* cake, my personal favorite, to carry out to the food cabinet at the counter. Delicious cheese cake meets the bakery, I made *Cassata alla Siciliana* from a recipe handed down from my grandmother, a staunch Sicilian who emigrated to New Zealand in pursuit of love as a young woman. She married her man and settled here, where my mum and I were born. It was my favorite of all the cakes and pies she had taught me how to make. And she'd taught me to make a few.

Sophie walked out into the café as she tied one of our Cozy Cottage pink aprons with the white polka dots around her slim waist. "Now, tell me all about the speed dating night. Did you meet Mr. Right?"

I pressed my lips together and shook my head.

"How about Mr. Right Now?"

I laughed, shaking my head once more. "Not even one of those."

"Oh well. Better luck next time." She shot me a breezy smile and powered up the coffee machine, ready for the early-bird customers who would come through the doors shortly, looking for their breakfast and first caffeine fix of the day.

"Oh, I won't be speed dating again, I can tell you that right now." My cheeks flushed as I thought of Reg the robot-maker, Fake Jamie Oliver slash Fabio—and Adam.

"Well, if that's the case," Paige said as she joined us at the counter to slide another freshly baked cake into the cabinet beside the *Cassata alla Siciliana*, "we need to come up with another way for you to go on your Last First Date."

"Hmmm." Although I'd agreed to this pact, I was having serious second thoughts about my chances of finding "The One," no matter how positive my friends were being for me. It all seemed too hard. "By my calculations, I had *four* Last First Dates at the speed dating thing. That's more than enough for anyone."

"You're in on that pact, too?" Sophie asked, her eyebrows raised.

"I am . . . or I was . . . Oh, I'm not sure." I scrunched up my face.

"Don't be put off, okay?" Paige put her hand on my arm. "You'll find him. Look at me? I thought Marcus was the man for me, until I realized it was Josh."

I glanced at her pretty face. I wished I had her blind optimism.

After my experience last night, I was more than happy to let the whole thing slide.

And anyway, the problem was, I *had* found him, I'd found "The One." Just over five years ago. In fact, I'd found him, and I'd kept him. Happily. It was the best thing I'd ever done with my life.

And I knew I'd wanted to be with him forever. Dan, my soulmate, my love. When he'd proposed, there was no question in my mind we were right for one another, that we belonged together. And we were so in love, so happy.

Until he was gone.

A chill came over me.

I'll never forget the moment I learned Dan had died in a horrific mountain biking accident. Dan, my fiancé. Dan, the guy who should have been my Last First Date, before any of us made the pact. We'd only been engaged for a matter of weeks, and then he was gone. Leaving me sad. Alone.

Broken.

Like Ryan.

I pasted on a smile. "You're right. I will."

Better to act like I agreed with her to avoid the inevitable plotting and planning I knew my friends were capable of. Heck, I'd plotted and planned to find Paige's Last First Date—and I'd got it right. Thanks to my matchmaking, Paige and Josh were now fully-carded members of "Happy Coupledom."

Maybe I was better at this for *other* people than I was for myself?

I glanced at the clock above the door. A handful of minutes to opening, but there were already a couple of men in business suits milling around out on the sidewalk.

"Are we ready to open up?" I asked the girls.

"Sure!" Paige wound her way around the counter and out through the café, extracting a key from a pocket under her apron as she walked. She pulled the door open. "Good morning, gentlemen. Come on in!"

And so the morning went, with our usual long line of customers drinking Ned's Coffee and eating their homemade meals, cakes, and snacks. We were always so busy, but it never felt like work to me.

I was putting paninis together to be toasted for the hungry lunch crowd due into the café in the next hour or so, when Paige stepped into the kitchen, her face beaming.

"What is it?" I asked with a smile.

"You have got to come out here."

I knitted my brows together. "Why? What's up?"

She took the tub of mozzarella from my hand, placed it on the kitchen counter, and handed me a clean cloth. "No questions. Just come."

Obediently, I wiped my hands and followed Paige out into the café and around the counter, where Sophie was serving a lone woman a slice of one of our cakes. We reached the table in the window where Cassie and Marissa were sitting.

"Hi, Cassie. Hi, Marissa." I smiled down at them.

"Sit," Paige commanded.

I pulled a chair out from the table and sat down. Once we were all seated, I looked between my friends' faces. "Okay, what's going on?"

"Cassie has news." Marissa's face was as bright as Paige's.

I turned my attention to Cassie. Her cheeks were flushed, framed by her long, auburn hair. Without a word, she lifted her left hand. My eyes were drawn instantly to the large, sparkling princess-cut solitaire diamond on her ring finger.

My jaw dropped open as I looked from the ring up into her eyes. "Did he . . .?"

She nodded, trying—and failing—to bite back a grin from bursting across her face, happiness emanating from her.

"When? How?"

"Last night, after the speed dating thing. I'm so sorry about that, by the way."

"Oh, forget about it. It was nothing. Now, let me get a look at that rock." I took her hand in mine and studied the ring. It was breathtakingly beautiful in its simplicity, a solitaire diamond in a platinum claw.

Will Jordan had outdone himself.

"That is gorgeous! And huge! Oh, Cassie, I'm so happy for

you." I leapt out of my chair and hugged her, surprising myself as tears sprang into my eyes. Tears of happiness—and something else.

Something I didn't want to think about.

"Did you two know?" I asked Marissa and Paige as I sat myself down once more, dabbing at my eyes with my fingers.

"It was a little hard for her to hide that rock. It's so big it could cause a total eclipse of the sun." Marissa grinned at her friend.

"To me, it was the look on her face the moment she walked through the café door that gave her away," Paige said, ever the romantic.

I glanced over at the counter. With Paige and I both sitting at the table, Sophie was left on her own. I didn't want to miss out on hearing all about Cassie's engagement, but we'd hit a quieter patch, with only a couple of customers waiting in line. I mouthed, "Are you okay?" and Sophie gave me the thumbs up.

I shot her a quick smile and returned my attention to Cassie. "Tell me everything. I need to live vicariously through you after my dating disasters last night."

"Well, I went to meet Will at about eight-thirty. I thought we were going out for a late dinner, as we sometimes do. Instead, he took me to the golf driving range we spent a lot of time at last year. You know, when I was trying to dazzle Parker with my nonexistent golfing expertise?"

We all laughed. There was no way Cassie was a born golfer.

"Oh, my God!" Paige exclaimed, her hand over her mouth. "The driving range is where you fell in love! Cassie, he is *so* romantic."

"I know," Cassie replied with a grin. "So, we got into the driving range and he purchased a tub of balls as usual. Then we went to our cubicle. I kept shooting him looks, because he was acting kinda weird, you know? But I figured he's pretty sports mad, so I just went with it."

"And?" Marissa was the least patient of all of us. "How did he do it?"

"Well, we each hit a few balls—or, he hit some, I missed most of mine," she added self-deprecatingly. "Then he asked me to get a pink ball out of the tub. It was the only pink one, and I hadn't noticed it before. I picked it up and spotted something strange about it, but I put it on the tee, all the same."

"The ring was in it?" Paige's voice was excited.

"Don't tell me you took a swing at it!" My eyes wide.

"Even if I had, I probably wouldn't have managed to hit it, anyway," Cassie replied with a laugh.

"True."

"And then, he asked me to open the ball. Of course, I looked at him like he was insane, but when I felt it, I could tell it wasn't a real ball. I flipped it open and saw this ring, sitting inside as though in a ring box." She held it up for us to admire once more.

"And Will was just standing there next to you?" Paige asked, riveted.

Cassie shook her head. "No. When I finally dragged my eyes from the ring, he was down on one knee."

"Oh, my." I placed my hand on my heart as Paige clapped her hands together again, and Marissa squealed.

Really, we were like a bunch of women in a Jane Austen novel, swooning at a gentleman's charming marriage proposal.

"What did he say?" Marissa asked. "Word for word."

"Well, he told me he loved me, that he couldn't imagine not being with me forever, and that he wanted to grow old with me, surrounded by our children and grandchildren."

In unison, we all let out an "Aww!"

"And then he took the ring out of the ball case, which he'd bought online somewhere. Apparently, there's a market for this sort of thing." She shrugged. "Who knew?"

"Then he slipped it on your finger, you said yes, and you had the most magical kiss of your life," Paige said.

"Yes, actually. That's exactly how it went."

I'd been holding my memories back, not allowing myself to think of my own proposal. But they pushed through, my mind darting to the moment Dan had presented me with a ring, when he'd uttered those four wonderful words I wanted to hear from him. *Will you marry me?*

We were on a weekend away in the Hawke's Bay region, the picturesque "fruit bowl of New Zealand." Although I wasn't much of a cyclist, we'd hired a couple of bikes and cycled along a path by the stunning Tuki Tuki River, past vineyards and orchards, out to a golden sand beach. On a picnic blanket in the shade of a beautiful, old pohutukawa tree, he pulled a small box out of his backpack, and presented me with the most exquisite ring I'd seen in my life. Ornate, old fashioned, perfect.

It was a precious memory—one I kept tucked away, safely inside. One I chose not to visit too often.

"I know it's only just happened, but you girls know you're going to be my bridesmaids, right?" Cassie said.

There were excited exclamations from the others at the table. I had to shake myself out of my memory and paste on a smile. "I would love to be a bridesmaid, thank you."

"Best. Bridesmaids. Ever," Cassie declared. "And there won't be any horrendous meringues or ugly bridesmaid dresses in sight. You will all look beautiful, I promise."

As the others talked about what sort of wedding Cassie wanted, I noticed the line of customers growing. I seized the chance to leave, so excused myself to go help Sophie.

Once I'd served up a slice of flourless chocolate and raspberry cake to the last in the line of customers, I opened the cabinet to rearrange what was left of our sweet treats and work out what we needed to replace before the lunchtime rush.

I let out a long sigh. I was happy for Cassie and Will. They were so good together, so right. Only . . . well, their happiness simply served to amplify my own loneliness—and the fact I once had what they have now.

My chest ached as I tried not to think about Dan.

After I'd said "yes" that day, we sat together on the picnic blanket, me leaning against him, both of us looking out to sea. We listened to the waves lapping at the shore, hearing the occasional squawk from a seagull overhead. We didn't need to rush to tell anyone we were engaged, we just wanted to *be*. Him and me, together, basking in our love, happy.

When I lost him, I lost that deep sense of contentedness I'd had, that feeling I belonged to someone. And he belonged to me.

More than anything, I wanted to have that feeling once more.

But now I was faced with the abject failure of the speed dating excursion Marissa was so certain would work for me. I was back to the drawing board.

It was just me and my memories of what I used to have.

"Hey there, speed dater," a masculine voice said, muffled by the fact my head was deep inside the cabinet.

I jerked up to see who it was and banged the top of my head on the edge of the cabinet. I let out a yelp as I pulled my head out, rubbing where it had made contact.

"Ow, that *had* to hurt."

I smiled, my face warming up as my tummy fluttered at the sight of the man on the other side of the counter.

Ryan.

Still looking like Thor.

Oh, my.

"Oh, it's nothing," I managed through my embarrassment.

"You really need to look out for those cabinets, you know. It's widely known they want to bring down the human race and make us all into their slaves."

I let out a laugh as I looked up into his warm hazel eyes. He was even more gorgeous today, his beard freshly clipped, his pale blue shirt setting off his dirty blond hair. "What . . . what can I get you?"

Say me, say me, say me.

"A double shot latte, thanks." He flashed his heart-stopping grin.

Darn it.

"Anything to go with that? We have a lot of different cakes."

He eyed the cabinet food, then shot me his grin once more. "I'll take a slice of that gourmet pizza there, thanks."

"No cake? Let me guess, you don't have a sweet tooth." I wanted to keep him talking, even if it was just about cake.

"Would you believe me if I said I was sweet enough?"

Sweet? Maybe. Hot? Definitely.

"That sounds a lot like one of those lines you mentioned last night."

"I've got more where that one came from." His smile reached his eyes, his features softened.

The effect was . . . well, I was forced to clear my throat. "Do you . . . ah, want that warmed up?"

"Sure."

I passed the coffee order on to Sophie, who was gazing at Ryan from behind the counter. "One double shot latte coming up," she said, her face flushing.

Geez. Between our matching blushes, we could probably heat the coffee with our cheeks.

He smiled at her but returned his gaze to me. "So, the speed dating was a bust?"

"Yeah. I think I'll just forget the whole thing."

"What? 'Give up on love?'" He used air quotes to emphasize his sarcasm.

I laughed. "Well, give up on speed dating, anyhow. Love? I'm still a believer."

He placed his elbow on the counter and leaned in toward me. His face a mere two feet from mine. My heart rate kicked up a notch or ten.

"Love sucks, and the sooner you learn that, the better off you will be. Take it from someone who knows."

I creased my brow, taken aback by his bitterness. "Oh. Right." I didn't know quite what to say. I mean, how did you respond to *that*?

Marissa materialized at his side, shooting me an enquiring look. I cast my eyes down, smoothing my apron over my full skirt. I took the opportunity to place the pizza slice on a plate and put it in the microwave to warm it up.

"Hey, brother. What are you doing here?" Marissa gave Ryan a quick hug.

"I was in the neighborhood and needed my caffeine fix. Don't worry, I know this is your girls' hang out. I'll get it to go." He turned to me and added, "If that's all right?"

"Sure," I replied, still reeling. The microwave beeped behind me, and I turned to bag up the pizza.

Sophie put the lid on his cup of coffee and handed it to him, grinning like a Cheshire cat.

Give it up, Sophie. He's anti-love.

I handed him his snack. "Here you are."

He took the paper bag and looked into my eyes once more. "Thanks, Bailey." He hesitated, his eyes on mine. "I'll, ah, see you 'round."

"Sure."

There was something in his gaze I couldn't read.

"Are you heading back to your office?" Marissa asked him, and he nodded. "I'll walk with you. Just give me a sec, okay?"

Ryan walked toward the door. I smiled at Marissa and turned to go back into the kitchen. I had cakes to restock, not hot men to feel conflicted over.

"Bailey?"

I turned back. "What's up?"

Marissa looked down at her hands and then back up at me. "I'm sorry about my brother."

"Don't be. He's fine," I lied.

"He's a work-in-progress."

"You mean the break-up?"

She nodded. "I think he's still messed up about women. She did a real number on him."

My heart softened. "Poor guy. It can be hard to get over someone."

She knitted her brows together. "Yeah."

The elephant in the room did a tap dance.

She paused, and then added in a brighter tone, "That's all I wanted to say. He can be a bit of a grump, thanks to Amelia breaking his heart like that."

Amelia. *Hmmm.* She had a lot to answer for.

"Don't worry about it." I shot her a smile and she appeared to be satisfied. "Do you spend a lot of your time apologizing for your brother?"

She shrugged. "I guess. Not as much as when she dumped him. He barely got off my sofa. But, hey, we've got much better things to focus on. Like being bridesmaids, right?"

My heart warmed at the thought. "Exactly."

"Look, Ryan's waiting for me, so I'd better go."

I looked out through the window and spotted Ryan's broad back, his face in profile as he looked up the street, take-out coffee and bag in hand. He'd put his sunglasses on in the bright morning sun. "'Kay. See you soon."

Marissa left the café, walking down the street with Ryan, and out of view.

After all this time alone, not wanting to even look at another guy, why did I have to go get feelings for someone who was more bitter than squeezed lemon?

And not only that, someone who showed zero interest in taking things any further with me than just flirting—as nice as it was?

I let out a puff of air. I was beginning to think it would be a million times easier just to stay single and forget this whole Last First Date thing.

Chapter 5

I PEERED OVER THE top of my laptop at Paige, trying to digest her latest business expansion idea. I'd learned since going into business with her that she had a lot of ideas. Some good, some borderline—some borderline insane.

I was trying to work out where this latest one lay.

"Don't you see how perfect this could be? Catering is the next logical step for the Cozy Cottage." Her face radiated enthusiasm.

"How would this work, exactly?" I closed my laptop, giving her my full attention.

"We would start off doing some small events, which we could advertise for on our website. We'd limit the menu to just a few dishes, finger food, desserts. You know, keep it simple."

"Paige, I'm not sure opening a catering business is exactly *simple*."

She pulled out a chair opposite me and sat down. The café was closed for the day, we'd completed the clean-up, and now I was trying to catch up on the accounts—the one thing I disliked about running the café. Paige's boyfriend, Josh, had helped me out, but I still struggled with crunching the numbers.

"I know it won't be simple, but we've got such a great brand."

"We do?"

I'd never thought about the Cozy Cottage as having a "brand." To me, it was just the Cozy Cottage—a place I loved to be.

"Yes! All that website stuff I put together reflects the feel of this place." She looked around the room. "All of that is our brand. And it's strong. Look at how busy we are every day. I think it's the perfect time for us to branch out."

I chewed on my lip. A lot of cafés also catered events, so it wasn't like we'd be doing something out of the ordinary. But the thought of taking a risk when I'd just got so comfortable with the way things were scared the living daylights out of me.

"Look." Paige placed her hands on the table. "How about I put a business plan together? I can work out costs, potential profit margins, that sort of thing. Then we can talk again?"

"I don't know, Paige. It sounds like a big risk to me. I like where we are right now. It's good, it works."

I wasn't sure why I was so reluctant. I mean, I'd made a huge change to the business by bringing Paige in as a partner, plus we'd introduced the Cozy Cottage Jam sessions, loved by local musicians and customers alike. We were on a high, and business had never been better.

But, for some reason, branching out into catering felt like a step too far for me.

Paige leant across the table and placed her hand on top of mine. "Bailey, let me show you how good this could be, okay?" Her face was so open, so full of hope.

Saying no to her right now would feel like punishing a puppy.

I shrugged. "Sure. I guess it can't hurt to see what you suggest."

She leant back in her chair, grinning. "Awesome! I'll work on it over the next few days. Once you can see how much sense it makes for us to do this, we can take on a client."

I raised my eyebrows. "A client?"

She nodded, biting back a smile. "Actually, I've already found us one."

"But—"

She interrupted me, her hand in the air in the "stop" sign.

"Before you say anything, it's not set in stone, but I know they're looking for a caterer."

"You didn't make a commitment to them that we'd do it, did you?"

She shook her head. "All I said was we would be in touch if we decide to go down this route. But, Bailey, I know we will. And it'll be *such* a success."

I couldn't help but smile at Paige and her infectious optimism. Maybe this was what I needed to pull me out of my reverie, to give me the kick in the pants to try something new?

And to take my mind off my Last First Date disaster.

"Okay. Pull something together for me, and we'll talk about it. That's all I'm committing to right now."

Paige squealed. "This is going to be so great, Bailey!"

I returned her smile. I hoped she was right.

THE FOLLOWING MORNING, at the same time he turned up yesterday—not that I'd been checking the clock, you understand—Ryan sauntered into the café. He was looking just as Norse god-like as he always did, his stride strong and purposeful as he walked straight up to the register where I was handing an older man his change.

"Thank you so much," I said to the man with a smile, training my eyes on him rather than where they were straining to go. "I'll bring your slice of cake over with your pot of Earl Grey tea when it's ready."

The man thanked me, turned, and walked over to a table.

I looked up at Ryan, doing my best to ignore the way in which my heart rate had kicked up a notch at the mere sight of him.

Really, this guy was bad for my cardiac health.

"Good morning, Ryan."

"Hey." One of his sexy smiles teased at the edges of his mouth. He turned to glance around the café.

I took the opportunity to take a deep breath to quell my nerves.

He turned back and flashed me his devastating smile. "No kid sister, so the coast is clear."

"Marissa's not usually here until ten or so."

"Good to know."

I shot him a sideways glance. "Are you avoiding her?"

"No. It's just this whole 'Cozy Cottage is a girls' hang out' thing she's got going on. You know, the no-men-allowed rule?"

"I sure do."

For as long as I'd known Marissa, Cassie, and Paige they had made my café their own with only one rule—no men. Sure, they could talk about them—which they had done, a lot—but they couldn't bring them here.

"What I don't understand is why their boyfriends are allowed here now, but not their dashingly handsome brothers." He shot me a cheeky smile.

I swear my legs could have buckled beneath me.

"Well, not that I'm telling tales or anything, but Marissa was in here yesterday afternoon with that new boyfriend of hers."

He crossed his arms, his eyes dancing. "Really?"

I laughed. "You didn't hear it from me, okay?"

"It's all fuel in the ongoing sibling battlefield."

I smiled at him. This was easy, fun. If I could only get the message through to my tingling body not to notice how hot he was, we could have an easy-going friendship.

Uncomplicated.

"What about you?"

"What do mean?"

"I mean, do *you* bring any men here?"

I blinked at him. Was he asking if I was still single? I'd have to have worked pretty fast since the speed dating evening if I wasn't.

"You mean other than the guy who thinks Reginald Whatshis-name is the most undervalued member of the Starship Enterprise?"

He laughed, shaking his head. "I *knew* he was your type."

I shrugged, enjoying our repartee. "How could I resist a geeky guy who wants to model his robot after me?"

"Well, he chose the perfect model."

Damn, flirting with him was fun. "Err, thanks." Heat bloomed once more in my cheeks.

"What can you recommend?"

For a moment I was confused, until I saw him nodding at the food in the cabinet at my side.

I cleared my throat. "Well, we have a lot of cakes, as you can see. Plus, we've got the pizza you had last time. Would you like that again?"

"Actually, I like the look of the cake stack thing there." He pointed at one of the cakes in the cabinet.

"Oh, that's the *Cassata alla Siciliana* cake."

"The cassa-what?"

I laughed. "*Cassata alla Siciliana*," I repeated, pronouncing it in Italian the way my grandmother, Nona, had taught me. "It's an Italian cake, a family recipe."

"Say it again," he said, his eyes sparkling as his face creased into a smile.

The heat in my cheeks turned red hot. We were back to flirting? "*Cassata alla Siciliana*."

"I could listen to you say that all day."

I shot him a sideways glance, trying to ignore the warmth spreading through my belly. "Shall I cut you a slice?"

"Oh, yeah. And a double shot latte. To eat in, since there's no bossy little sister here to shoo me away."

"Coffee and cake coming right up."

He paid, a shot of electricity jolting through me when my fingers brushed his as I handed him his change—just to make it all the more awkward for me. He wandered over to sit down in one of the comfy armchairs by the fireplace.

It was late summer, so the fire wasn't burning, but in winter it was one of my favorite spots in the whole café. A hot drink, a slice of cake, and a cozy, glowing fire. Bliss.

The café was quiet before the rush, Sophie was on her break, and Paige was never very good at running our behemoth coffee machine, so I made Ryan's coffee and took it and his cake over to him. I placed them both down on the table by his chair.

"Enjoy!" I turned to leave, half hoping he would invite me to sit with him so I could gaze into those eyes once more.

The other half reminded me he was totally embittered about women, and I would do well to stay far, far away.

In the end, I didn't have to make a choice. He simply thanked me and turned his attention to his phone.

I returned to the counter, feeling ridiculous once again.

Why did I have such a crush on this guy? Because that was all it was—a crush. Although he was a little flirty when we talked, he had made it clear he wasn't looking for anything from me.

I guess all I could do was sit and wait, hoping my feelings would die a natural death to put me out of my misery.

Oh, but that Ryan Jones did not play fair.

He came in at the same time again the next day and the day after that, ordering the *Cassata alla Siciliana* and a cup of coffee each time. He was always a little flirty, his smile enough to make my heart rate quicken and my cheeks blush.

And then, on the fourth day, he didn't show.

Despite telling myself not to, I kept checking the clock, wondering whether he was running late, wondering if he was going to show. By the end of the lunchtime rush, there was still no sign of him. I couldn't help but feel let down, like seeing him was one of the highlights of my day—even if it was clear he didn't return my feelings.

To him, I was just the girl at the café, welcoming him with a ready smile, an embarrassing blush, and a touch of flirtatious banter. The girl who delivered him his caffeine and sugar fix.

And me wanting more from him wasn't going to change that.

Chapter 6

"AND THAT, DEAR BAILEY, is how we are going to take Auckland's catering world by storm!" Paige thumped to the table with her palm to emphasize her point.

I had to smile. She'd put together an elaborate presentation, complete with stats, a detailed business model, and even embedded videos, all to showcase how amazing and successful she believed "Cozy Cottage Catering" would be.

Her enthusiasm was infectious, and I was finding it hard to fault her approach—as nervous as I was about branching out like this.

When I didn't say anything, Paige looked like she might explode. "So? What do you think?"

"I think you've put forward a really compelling case."

She waved her hand in the air. "Oh, forget about that. Do you want to do it or not?"

I scrunched up my nose. I was so reticent about trying this. I was beginning to second-guess my judgment. I mean, I was thirty years old, and I had a *crush* on a guy.

I let out a puff of air, regarding Paige's hopeful expression.

I thought about how I'd opened the Cozy Cottage, how I'd taken a punt on myself, not knowing whether I'd succeed. And I had succeeded, loving the place I'd created, never once regretting it.

Perhaps I just needed to go for it? Try something new?

"Maybe we could give it a shot?" I ventured.

She literally jumped for joy, right out of her seat. "Yes!" She pulled me in for a hug. "Oh, Bailey, this is going to be *such* a success, I can totally feel it."

I laughed. "I hope you're right."

"I know I am. Okay, let's get down to it. I'll get some business cards made up, I'll update the website with some info on us, and why don't we sit down and work out a potential list of dishes?"

"That sounds like we're totally throwing ourselves into this."

"I guess. But nothing ventured, nothing gained, right?"

I decided to surrender myself to Paige's enthusiasm. It was really the only way—she was like a hormonal woman searching for a chocolate fix when she got a new idea. Sometimes, I wondered how Josh coped.

"I guess you're right."

"Awesome! Together, we can meet with this potential client, too. How's Saturday for you after closing? Sound good?"

I thought of my date-free Saturday nights and nodded. In fact, I was beginning to enjoy the way Paige's positivity was filling the room. "Sounds good. Who's the client?"

"You'll have to wait and see." She flashed me a smile, waggling her eyebrows.

We spent the next hour going about the everyday tasks we had to do at the end of a working day: placing orders, discussing menus, checking staff rosters, and ensuring the café was in excellent condition to open up tomorrow morning, and do it all again.

As I walked around the kitchen counter to lock up, there was a rap on the door. Josh poked his head around the side.

"Bailey!" he said with his characteristic grin as he stepped into the kitchen. He pulled me in for a hug, as though he hadn't seen me for weeks.

I saw him yesterday.

I'd known Josh for a long time, and we'd grown close over the years. He may have been Dan's little brother, but he was like a *big* brother to me, over the last few years. He was always looking out for me and my best interests, right down to suggesting Paige as a potential new business partner.

I suppose Josh felt responsible for me after Dan's death, taking me under his wing, helping me launch the Cozy Cottage through his coffee company, Ned's Coffee, named in honor of his brother. You see, Josh couldn't pronounce "Dan" as a little boy, so he called him "Ned." Weird, I know, but the name kinda stuck.

I never called Dan "Ned," but serving Ned's Coffee at the café each day had kept Dan's memory alive—a daily reminder of the wonderful man he was, and what we'd had together.

When Josh told me he'd fallen in love with Paige some time back, I was so thrilled for him, despite the fact she had shown zero interest in him at that time. But I knew Josh was the kind of guy who just grew on you, and it was only a matter of time before Paige would realize what a special person he was. Which she did, of course, falling head over heels for him, too. They deserved one another—and the happiness they now had.

"Hey, Josh." He smiled at me and looked so much like Dan, my heart almost stopped. I had to catch my breath.

And then, as quickly as it had happened, he was back to Josh again. My heart returned to normal, a familiar brick of sadness settling in my belly.

I guess you could say it was a double-edged sword having Josh around.

Most days, I was fine, and life was good. I loved running the Cozy Cottage with Paige, I lived in a beautiful city, surrounded by good friends and family. But lately I've wanted more. I knew Dan was gone, but looking around at my friends and how happy they all were in love—even the former anti-commitment queen, Marissa—I wanted to be with someone. I wanted that deep happiness you get from being with someone you love, the feeling that it's you and him against the world, together.

But, so far, all I had were some crummy dates that went

nowhere and a crush on a guy who only wanted to flirt with me while he waited for his coffee order to be filled.

Not exactly shooting for the stars here.

"Did you have a good day?" Josh asked.

"Yes, actually." I smiled at him. "Paige and I have agreed to give catering a shot."

"Oh, that's so cool! She'll be so happy." He spied Paige out in the café, and a warm smile spread across his face. He walked past me and out of the room to greet her, and I turned away to slip on my jacket, not wanting to intrude on their private moment.

With my purse slung over my shoulder, I locked the back door, switched the lights off, and walked through to the café.

"All set?" Paige was standing arm in arm with Josh, looking like the cat who'd got the cream.

"Yes. I'll get here a little earlier tomorrow to bake. Our cakes have been super popular this week, have you noticed?"

"That's because they're the best cakes in Auckland city," Josh said.

I laughed. "You have to say that. You're in love with one of the bakers."

"Yeah." He smiled down at Paige, who blushed, grinning back up at him.

I walked to the front door, keys in hand. Sure, I was happy for them, but all this lovey-dovey stuff could get a little much.

Locking the door behind us, we walked down the street—me to catch my bus home, Josh and Paige to Josh's car parked nearby. As we passed by the store next to the café, I noticed there were boxes in the window where once there were beautiful floral displays and a host of gifts.

"What's going on with the florist?" I asked.

"I think they're going out of business," Paige replied. She turned to Josh. "Didn't you say that when you got me those gorgeous lilies last week?"

"Yeah. I think she said she was closing up shop sometime this week."

Huh. I'd clearly had my head so deeply buried in my own life, I'd failed to notice what was going on in my neighbor's life. Addison, the florist, was a sweet woman I'd spoken to a few times but had never gotten to know well. She'd only opened the store a few months ago, and florist work was as busy as running a café. I wondered what was going on with her to be closing up shop.

Josh and Paige continued walking, and I called out, "I'm going to say hi. See you guys tomorrow."

"Sure. Have a good night."

I knocked tentatively on the glass front door, which was standing ajar, some stacked boxes holding it open. "Hello?"

"Just a sec!" came a muffled voice from out back.

"No worries, Addison! It's just Bailey from the café next door."

As I waited, I looked around what had once been a pretty florist shop with tubs of flowers, potted plants, and assorted gifts, including the cutest teddy bears holding balloons that declared things like "It's a boy!" and "Congratulations!" They were all gone now, replaced with stacks of packing boxes.

"Hey, Bailey. Great to see you." Addison entered the shop from out back. She wiped her hands on her dark blue apron and smiled at me. "I guess you can tell I'm leaving."

I nodded. "What's happened?"

She shrugged, her face breaking out in a smile. "I fell in love."

"That's wonderful, but is it any reason to close up shop?"

"He lives in Orlando."

"*Orlando*? As in the Florida Orlando? In the US?"

She nodded, grinning. "I'm moving to Florida!"

Another woman about my age, fallen in love and changing her life. I tried not to think about it.

I stepped over some florist paraphernalia to give her a congratulatory hug. "That's such exciting news."

"Thanks. His name is John, and he's amazing. I think he's 'the one.'"

I returned her smile. She was uprooting her life to move half way around the globe for this guy. I hoped he was "the one," too—for her sake.

"Now, if you know anyone who wants to take over the lease on this place, I'd be really grateful. It's got a long time to run."

I glanced around the shop. "It's a good size. Not too large, not too small." I spied a familiar looking set of double wooden doors. "Hey, do those doors lead through to my café?"

"Sure do. Weird to think we've been separated by a couple of doors all this time, and didn't really know one another well. Apparently, your café and this shop used to be one big restaurant back in the 'eighties."

"I had no idea."

"Did you know there's a gorgeous covered courtyard out back, too?"

I raised my eyebrows. "There is?"

"Come with me."

I followed her past the counter, through her stock room, and into a quaint courtyard lined with ferns and other plants. There were cobblestones on the ground, and a trickling waterfall against the far wall. A small, rusty wrought iron table with two chairs sat in the middle, a couple of empty Ned's Coffee cups on top, no doubt from my café.

I put my hand over my heart as I took it all in. "Addison, this is gorgeous!"

"I know, right? I had plans to make this into an area for small outdoor plants, but," she shrugged, "that's not going to happen now."

"When do you go?"

"Next week."

"So soon?"

She nodded, her smile not dropping for a second.

I pulled her in for another hug. "Well, I wish you the best of luck."

We walked back through the backroom and out into the shop.

"I've got a long night of packing and organizing ahead. I'll stop by for a coffee and say 'bye before I go, 'kay?"

"I'm going to hold you to that. Coffee and cake, on the house."

"Your cakes are to die for."

She was right, the Cozy Cottage cakes were pretty darn good, if I did say so myself. "Thanks, Addison."

"Call me Addi. Even though I'm leaving," she added with a laugh. "Hey, what's your number? I'll let you know how it all works out."

We exchanged contact info and said our goodbyes. I walked down the busy street to my bus stop. A long journey through rush hour later—that will teach me not to stop and chat to neighboring florists leaving town for love—and I walked the two blocks to my house.

I'd been lucky enough to inherit my place from my nona when she passed away seven years ago. She'd lived in it with my grandfather, my nonno, for more than forty-five years, raising their family. She was living in a once-foreign country she learned to call home, though she never lost her passion for Italy. The cooking smells that greeted us at the front door each time we came to visit never failed to make my mouth water.

Nona taught me to cook, to bake, to have a passion for food. I owed her so much, and I missed her every day of my life.

I pushed my white wooden gate open and stepped into my modest front yard, hearing the gate creak. I needed to remember to oil that, and although it'd been creaking for at least a year, it wasn't on my list of priorities.

Walking up my brick pathway and through the front door, I let out a relieved breath of air as I dropped my purse on the hallway table. I shrugged off my jacket and kicked off my high heeled shoes, my toes thanking me for their emancipation, cooled by the hardwood floors.

I loved shoes, especially a great pair of heels. Next to food, they were my favorite things, and I could almost rival the famous Imelda Marcos in the number I owned. In fact, I had converted the smallest bedroom in the house into a closet, my shoes lining the walls, a soft ottoman placed in the middle of the room where I sat each morning to slip them on once I'd chosen which pair I would wear for the day.

I padded into my bedroom, reaching behind myself to unzip my dress. This part was always tricky and I wondered, not for the first time, whether I should attach a piece of long string to my zippers to make unzipping my snug-fitting dresses easier. You needed "hacks' like that when you lived alone.

Finally managing to unzip my dress, I stepped out of it and slipped on a tank top and pair of jean shorts. I pulled the tie out of my long dark hair and ruffled my hair, my curls falling over my shoulders.

Although I adored my fifties-inspired clothes for work, when I was home, I was strictly a comfort-first girl, eschewing the nipped in waists that contained my hour-glass figure so well. No one was here to see me, so what did it matter?

I glanced in the mirror, casting a critical eye over myself. Although I wasn't an eighteen-year-old stick insect with a tiny, perky chest and boyish hips—almost the opposite, in fact—I didn't think I looked too bad. Sure, my workwear enhanced my assets and hid my thighs, but I looked good enough in my shorts.

So why couldn't I find a great guy to date? I was good enough looking, I ran my own business, I didn't do mean things to kittens.

Heck, *I'd* date me.

Now, all I needed to do was find a guy who a) didn't want to use me as a prototype for a robot, or b) think he was God's gift to women.

Hmm. A much harder task than I'd first thought.

There was a knock at my front door, interrupting my pity party. In my bare feet, I padded down the hall. Through the textured glass, I could see a tall person, probably a man, standing on my doorstep.

I furrowed my brow. I wasn't expecting anyone.

"Who is it?" I called as my phone rang in the other room.

"It's Ryan . . . Ryan Jones," a muffled voice replied.

Ryan? *Here?*

My tummy was in knots and my excitement rose inside as a thousand questions slammed into my brain.

What was he doing here?

Had he changed his mind about me?

Why did I have to be dressed in shorts?

"Just a second!" I was stalling for time.

I glanced in the mirror above the small table in the hallway. Even though I'd only just been putting myself through a body assessment in my bedroom, I hadn't been looking for whether my nose was shiny or my mascara smudged. They were, both of them.

A quick under-eye sweep and nose-blot later, I clenched my hands at my sides, taking a deep breath before I pulled the door open. His back was turned as he looked down the street. And then, just like a leading man in a Hollywood movie, he looked over his shoulder and into my eyes.

You know that expression "my heart leapt into my mouth?" Well, that's what it did, right then and there.

"W-what are you doing here?" I completely failed to compose myself before I spoke.

"I was in the neighborhood and remembered you live here. You know, from that time with Marissa?"

I nodded, recalling how Marissa had dropped by with Ryan and Nash a couple weeks back—and how I'd wished I'd been wearing some cute outfit instead of shorts and a tank that day, too.

"I can leave, if now's not a good time?" he added uncertainly. "I know most people text first."

"No, no!" It was quite possible I sounded a little too eager.

Be relaxed, easy-going.

Yeah, like guys like Ryan Jones turn up on my doorstep every day of the week.

Only, they so didn't.

I cleared my throat. "Umm, would you like to come in? I just got home and was going to fix a drink."

His face creased into a heart-stopping cute smile. "A drink sounds great."

As I stood back and he stepped over the threshold into my house, I couldn't help but hope he was here for me. That somehow, he was over the ex who had hurt him so badly, and he was ready for . . . for what?

As I closed the door behind me, I shot him a nervous smile.

Perhaps it was my turn, after all?

Chapter 7

"THIS IS SUCH A great place," Ryan said as he looked around my living room.

I glanced around self-consciously, wishing I'd known he was coming so I could have had the chance to straighten the place up, maybe have thrown a cloth or a vacuum cleaner around.

But guys didn't notice that kind of thing, right?

Well, I hoped they didn't, anyway.

"Thanks." I spied a pair of shoes I'd kicked off last night as I collapsed on the sofa after a long day at the Cozy Cottage. I surreptitiously shoved them under the sofa with my foot.

"What can I get you?" I did a quick mental inventory of my refrigerator. "I've got beer, some wine, juice . . . maybe milk?"

Milk? I just offered the first hot guy to cross my threshold in a long time milk?

Smooth, Bailey.

His smile didn't falter. "Although milk sounds great, I might go for a beer."

"Beer. Of course. You are a grown up." I let out a laugh. "Be right back." My face heated up as I turned and walked into my kitchen. Opening the refrigerator door, I hoped the cool air might counteract the pinkness I knew must be blooming in my cheeks. I reached in, grabbed a couple bottles of beer, and returned to him.

"Here." I handed him one of the cold bottles.

"Thanks."

We stood next to one another in silence. What should I say? Him turning up like this had totally flustered me. I lifted my beer to my lips and *clunk!* The metal cap clattered against my teeth. "Ow!"

"Yeah, you might want to open that first," he said with a chuckle. "You okay?"

My cheeks turned nuclear. If I could have fallen through a hole in the floor right then, I would have done it. Gladly.

"I'm fine. I'll go get a bottle opener."

"Great idea."

I beat a hasty retreat back to the kitchen. Locating the opener in a top drawer, I scrunched my eyes shut for a moment.

I really needed to get a grip!

Sure, he was good looking, fun and sexy, and he definitely had an effect on me. Those eyes, those wide shoulders, the way his shirt hinted at a firm, muscular torso beneath. I let out a sigh. I was a thirty-year-old woman, not some teenager with her first crush.

I could handle Ryan Jones.

Hot he may be, but this was not my first rodeo.

Back in my living room, Ryan was peering at my collection of framed photos sitting on the mantelpiece above my exposed brick fireplace. With his back to me once more, I ran my eye over what he was wearing—a casual but stylish ensemble of a collared checked shirt, sleeves rolled up, a pair of cargo shorts, which showed off his long, muscular legs, and a pair of white sneakers on his feet.

Casually-dressed Thor on a day off from his divine duties.

I cleared my throat. "Here you go." I reached out and he handed me his bottle. I flipped the cap off, catching it in my free hand, then did the same with mine.

"Who's this? Is it you?" He pointed at the largest photo in the assortment.

I looked at the picture in the old, wooden frame, warmth spreading through my belly at the memory. "Yeah. That's me with my nona when I was about six."

"You were cute. Totally rocking those pigtails." He shot me a smile. "One question, though. What's a nona?"

I laughed. "Grandma. It's Italian. She's Italian. *Was*. She . . . she died a few years back."

He returned his attention to the photo. "She looks like she was a nice woman."

"She was. She was the best. Barely spoke English, but she taught me how to cook."

I thought of how I would stand on a little stool at the kitchen counter, Nona showing me how to knead bread, how to crack eggs, how to beat butter and sugar. Out of nowhere, I felt a pang of sadness for her loss. She had always been there, only a few streets away from my childhood home, a constant presence in my life from as far back as I could remember.

"So she's why you can speak Italian so well?"

I nodded.

He raised his bottle. "Here's to you and Nona." Ryan clinked his bottle against mine.

I smiled at him. Hot *and* sweet? Jackpot.

He returned to my photo collection once again. Before I could stop him, he picked up a picture of Dan and me taken the day we got engaged.

I swallowed, that recurring brick growing to my belly.

This was beyond weird.

He examined the photo in his hands. "Is that Josh?"

I forced a smile. "No, that's Dan . . . he's . . . *was* Josh's brother." I held my breath.

The last man who I had been alone in this room with was Dan. Now Ryan was here, and it felt . . . I don't know. Wonderful? Yes, but definitely something else at the same time.

"Right." He placed the picture back with the others. "You have a nice place here. I already said that. Sorry."

I let out a light laugh, sensing his nerves matched mine, glad we were moving on from the dead fiancé conversation.

"Thank you. Would you like to sit down? I mean, unless you want to stand? I know sitting is the new smoking, right?"

"I'd heard that." She didn't move.

"Right. And smoking causes cancer, and no one wants cancer."

Cancer?

"Sit, stand. Totally up to you, of course."

Someone stop me. Please!

His face creased into a smile. "Sure. I'd like to sit, even with the increased risk of cancer."

"Great." As I sat down on my sofa, I scrunched my eyes shut. First milk now cancer? *Geez, Bailey.*

Ryan took a seat in an armchair opposite me. "So, did your nona help you set up the Cozy Cottage?"

"No, she died before I got that place. I . . . ah, opened the place up with someone else."

The elephant in the room's name was Dan. He and I had fallen in love with the idea of owning a café together, of making it into the kind of place we liked to go. The Cozy Cottage was our dream—only, he never got to experience it like I did.

I wrung my hands in my lap. Why was I thinking about Dan?

"But I like to think Nona's watching over me. I think she'd be happy with how I've chosen to live my life, you know, running a café, around food all day, every day."

I took another swig of my beer, and another. After the alcohol hit my bloodstream, I began to feel more relaxed.

Whoever invented alcohol must have known how it could help in situations like this. Like when your crush turns up at your place unexpectedly, you think about your former fiancé, and you start to talk about cancer. That sort of situation.

"I bet your nona's really proud of you. You're . . . you're great."

My eyes darted to his face. He was gazing directly at me, an intensity in his eyes I hadn't seen before.

Something shifted between us.

"I . . . thanks." I smiled, not letting my eyes drop from his. Part of me willed him to keep looking at me with those warm, hazel eyes of his. Another part had my insides twisted up, that photo of me and Dan burning a hole in my heart.

Ryan blinked and looked down, the moment between us over. He cleared his throat. "So, I've got a new place."

"You do? No more sleeping on Marissa's sofa?"

Ryan had been at Marissa's apartment since he'd broken up with his ex. Getting his own place was a move in the right direction for him.

"As comfortable as that was." He laughed. "It's not far from here, actually. On Dorchester Street."

I thought of the leafy street with its cute cafés and boutiques. "Nice. When did you move in?"

"About two weeks ago. It's good to have my own space again. Marissa was over me staying with her, especially now that she's all loved up with Nash."

I studied his face. His expression was not one of admiration.

"Yeah, they seem really happy."

He harrumphed in response.

I creased my brow. "You don't like Nash?"

Nash was one of the nicest guys I'd met, and he was so clearly in love with Marissa. How anyone couldn't like him was beyond me.

"No, he's great. It's not that, it's just . . . *love*." He pulled a face. "You know?"

I nodded, not "knowing" in the least. To me, love was the pinnacle—what we were all looking for, what we all wanted in this life.

What I'd had with Dan.

Not something to pull a face over.

"Right." It was best to change the topic of conversation. Work had to be an easier subject. I took another swig of my beer, the bubbles tickling my nose. "So, you're an architect, right?"

His expression changed as he nodded. "Yeah, I work for Accent Architecture. I've been there since college. We've been pretty busy, actually. We even just hired a new intern."

I sat and listened. He was clearly passionate about his work, and I was drawn to him all the more. A man who loved what he did, who was creative and committed to his career, was pretty darn sexy in my eyes. The fact he looked the way he did was just the icing on the cake.

"We're working on that tech guy's new place right now. Down on Cremorne Street."

"Isn't Cremorne Street the most expensive street in Auckland?"

"One of them, maybe? It's pretty nice."

"Impressive."

"How about you?"

"I'm not looking to build a multi-million-dollar mansion anytime soon," I replied with a smile.

"I could give you a discount. You know me." He winked and shot me a cheeky grin.

I responded with a quizzical smile. Was he flirting with me again?

Man, I could not work this guy out! On the one hand, he talked about how anti-love he was, and on the other, he'd been flirting with me for a while now, and had just turned up on my doorstep.

Talk about a hot conundrum.

"What I meant was, is running a café what you always wanted to do? Is it your passion?"

"Actually, it is. I've always loved cooking and baking, and . . . people, I guess. Doing something that involved all three seemed like a good idea. And now I have Paige who knows so much about marketing and business. It's a match made in heaven."

"Well, I don't have much of a sweet tooth, but that cake you suggested is really good. Which is why I've kept ordering it."

"A Nona special." I smiled at him, enjoying getting to know him a little better—and the fact he liked my baking made me want to smile all day long, too.

We sat in silence for a while, drinking our beer. I noticed he kept shifting his feet as though he couldn't get comfortable.

He drained his beer, placing the bottle on the coffee table. "Well, I guess I should get going." He stood up. It was abrupt and unexpected.

"Okay," I replied, startled. I stood up, too.

"Thanks for the beer."

"No problem."

"Do you want me to . . .?" He nodded at the kitchen.

"No, no. I'll get them."

"'Kay." He paused, his gaze moving from me to the wall and then back to me again. He looked torn, lost almost.

I watched him closely. *What is going on with him?*

After a beat, he looked down and pulled his car key fob from his pocket. "I'll . . . ah, I'll see you 'round." He shot me a quick smile then turned and walked toward the door.

I hesitated, knitting my brows together. I followed, holding the door for him once he'd pulled it open and stepped out onto the welcome mat.

He turned back to face me. "Thanks."

"Sure." I smiled through my confusion. "It was nice to see you again."

"Yeah." His eyes bored into me. He paused for a beat, two. "I . . ." He inched closer to me, and my eyes instinctively dropped to his lips.

I swallowed, my nerves kicking up a notch.

Is he going to . . . kiss me?

I looked from his lips back up into his eyes, creeping closer to him, my breath catching in my throat. I wanted to reach out and touch him, feel his lips on mine.

But instead, in a fraction of a heartbeat, he blinked and backed away from me.

The moment—if it even was a moment—was gone.

"I'll see you later." He concentrated on the floor by my feet.

"Sure. See you later."

He turned and walked down the path. He paused, looked back, and half-smiled. It seemed forced, sad somehow. He turned and walked down to the gate then disappeared up the street.

I closed the door, deep in thought. He'd turned up here and looked like he was going to kiss me. And then . . . nothing.

I couldn't help but feel he wanted more, that he was *here* for more.

But then again, maybe I'd imagined the whole thing?

Chapter 8

AFTER RYAN AND THE possible "almost kiss" last week, questions had pinged around my brain like a bucket of table tennis balls let loose in a wind tunnel.

He'd flirted just enough to make me think he liked me, but had pulled back before anything had happened. Then there was the way he'd referred to love, like it was a four-letter word or something.

Which it was, of course. But not in *that* way.

Did it mean he wasn't over his ex? Had she scarred him so much he no longer believed in love? Or was it just some throw-away comment, a guy thing I would never get?

So many questions, so few answers. *Not* my preferred ratio.

In the end, I made the call I wasn't going to try to work him out. If he had something he wanted to say to me, I would simply have to wait until he was ready.

And if he wanted to kiss me? Well, I'd just have to wait for that, too.

As much as it killed me.

Arriving at the café while the birds were waking up to catch those early worms on Saturday, I noticed Addi's florist shop was now totally empty. She was off on her adventure, following her heart to Orlando. I hoped it worked out for her. Moving to another hemisphere to be with someone was a big call.

I peered in the window. The flowers and pot plants were gone, even all the boxes, leaving an empty space. Suddenly inexplicably sad, I hoped Addi would find someone to take over her lease soon, to give this cute shop with the gorgeous courtyard a new lease on life. It deserved to be full of life, not empty and alone like it was right now.

Hold on. What was I thinking? It was a *shop*, not a living, breathing thing.

I filed "weird feelings about empty shop next door" away and unlocked the Cozy Cottage. Every day was a busy day at the café, and I had cakes to bake and coffee to brew.

I didn't have any time to moon over men—or empty shops.

Later that day, Sophie and I were cleaning up after the lunch rush when Paige called me over to her laptop, which she'd set up on one of the kitchen counters.

"I have something to show you." There was evident pride in her voice. She rotated her laptop so I could see the screen.

I studied it. It was a new page on our website entitled "Cozy Cottage Catering." She'd used the same fonts and layout as the rest of the site, and added a photo of one of our trademark pink aprons with white polka dots. It was folded neatly beside a plate of hors d'oeuvres, all sitting on top of a rustic wooden table. The styling was perfect and totally "on-brand," as I was learning to say.

"Oh, Paige," I exclaimed, impressed once again with her handiwork. "That looks amazing. I love it!"

She beamed at me. "It's not live yet. I wanted to get your go-ahead before I clicked the button."

"I can't imagine it looking more—" I examined the page as tried to find the word. Eventually, I landed on the feeling it gave me. "—right, I suppose."

"I wanted to stick with what we were trying to achieve. You know, simple, good, honest food with a touch of our Cozy Cottage magic."

"Well, you nailed it, chickadee. Let me have a quick look through it. Did you stick with the food plan?"

We had made a list of the types of dishes we thought we could make. Nothing too complex, simply good food, with an Italian twist. The list had made our mouths water as we'd compiled it. We were die-hard foodies, that's for sure.

"Of course. See?" She clicked on a tab that read "Menus."

Studying the list, I noticed it was all there, just as we'd agreed.

"And here's the pricing section." She clicked on another tab. "And our contact info, with a form for prospective clients to complete." The screen had boxes for people's names, email addresses, and the type of event they were planning. "If it all works the way it's meant to, every time someone fills in this form, we'll get an email. I've never done this type of work on a website before, but I watched some YouTube clips on how to do it. I think it's worked out pretty good."

The grin on my face was wide when I turned to Paige. "It's perfect. I know I couldn't have ever done anything like this."

"Thanks. I'm no web expert, but I've learned a few things."

"We're really doing this, aren't we?"

She returned my grin. "We are."

A host of emotions raced through me, from nerves to excitement and everything in between.

Paige pulled her phone out of the front pocket of her Cozy Cottage Café apron and scrolled through it. "You might remember I've scheduled a meeting with our first clients for—" She looked up at me with a glint in her eye. "—right about now."

I furrowed my brow. I recalled her mentioning an appointment with our first potential clients, but it had slipped my mind. "But, Paige, we're about to close up for the day."

She shrugged in response. "Sophie? You on it?"

She walked past us with a tray in her hands. "Totally on it."

"See? Come with me. They should be here by now." She closed her laptop and walked around the counter and out into the café. It was emptying out with no customers at the counter, just the few late-lunch stragglers we often got on a Saturday. I followed her to a table in the window.

When I spotted the two faces beaming at me, everything fell into place.

I let out a happy sigh, shaking my head. "Cassie and Will. *You're* our first ever catering customers?"

Cassie's grin was so broad, she looked like her face could crack in two. Her eyes roved from me to Will and back again. "If that's okay with you?"

"Are you kidding? Of course it's okay!" They stood up, their chairs scraping across the hardwood floors. I hugged them both, wondering how we'd manage to be bridesmaids *and* cater the wedding. We were going to need to invoke some sort of superpowers that day.

"That's good to hear. We don't have a Plan B," Will said.

Paige and I sat down at the table with the happy couple.

"As soon as Paige told us you were going to do this, we just knew we wanted you to cater our wedding," Cassie said.

Will nodded his agreement. "Although the deal is, I help choose the food and you do everything else, right, honey?"

Cassie shook her head, laughing. "Don't forget you've got to turn up on the day, too."

"Gotcha." He gave her a wink.

"Look at them, Bailey. The first of our pact to marry her Last First Date." Paige put her hand over her heart. "And *we* get to be a big part of it. This could not be more perfect."

"That's true." Cassie gazed at her beloved, who returned her smile tenfold.

My neck became stiff. As good as Paige and I were at running the café, even branching out into light dinners and wine for our Cozy Cottage Jam sessions, we hadn't ever catered an event before, let alone a wedding. Doing Cassie and Will's was like we were trying to compete at the Olympics before we'd even begun to crawl.

I put my hand on Cassie's arm. "Are you sure? We're brand new at this, and we'd hate to mess things up for you."

"We have faith in you. And you won't mess it up," Cassie

replied. "You know the Cozy Cottage has always been special to us."

"Yup," Will agreed, giving his fiancée's hand a squeeze. "I think Cassie fell for me when she found out this was my favorite café. I passed some kind of 'chick test,' right, Dunny?"

Cassie hit him playfully on the arm. "You said you weren't going to use that terrible nickname anymore. I don't like being called 'toilet' in Australian, thank you very much, *Poop Boy*."

Paige and I laughed. Will had abbreviated Cassie's last name, Dunhill, to "Dunny" a long time ago, and she'd retaliated with an equally terrible toilet-themed name for him. With the amount of ribbing they gave one another at the time, we should have known they would end up in love.

That level of teasing is often accompanied by some serious electricity.

Cassie turned back to me. "You have to make the cake. I know exactly what I want, too."

"Let me guess," Paige interrupted. "Chocolate and raspberry flourless cake, by any chance?"

Cassie grinned, her eyes dancing. "You know me too well."

"To be fair, it's all you've ever eaten here. In fact, without you, we'd be left with half a cake at the end of every day," I replied with a chuckle. "Now that I think about it, it's a miracle you're not the size of a house!"

The four of us girls were certainly creatures of habit when it came to cake. Cassie's favorite was our flourless raspberry chocolate cake, Paige's was carrot cake with cream cheese frosting, Marissa's was the orange and almond syrup cake, and mine was *Cassata alla Siciliana*. All Nona's recipes, all totally delicious.

"Well, you can't have too much of a good thing," Cassie replied. "But for our wedding cake, we'd actually like to go more traditional."

I raised my brows. "You would?"

Cassie shot Will a smile. "Yeah. My mum and dad kept their wedding cake and had a small slice every year. I think it's romantic."

"A traditional fruit cake then, huh?" I asked.

Cassie nodded. "Can you make that?"

Paige laughed. "You're asking the queen of cakes if she can make a fruit cake?"

I smiled as I thought of the fruit cake Nona and I had made each year for Christmas. Although she made the tradition Italian cake, *Pannetone*, as well, she had this idea that guests In New Zealand would prefer the traditional fruit cake. So bake it we did. "Yeah, I can. I've got just the recipe."

A group of late-lunch seekers entered the café, and Paige and I bid farewell to the happy couple to tend to the new patrons. Between the usual daily café business, we spent the rest of the day talking about the new catering business and thinking up ideas for Cassie and Will's wedding. Sophie was a godsend, as usual, satisfying customer's often elaborate coffee requests. Half caf, full cream, low foam, high foam, soy milk, caramel syrup.

I mean, whatever happened to ordering just a plain old cup of coffee?

The last customer served, we closed for the day. Paige and I sat down to finalize the website details before we went "live."

"Ready?" Paige's finger was poised over the mouse.

"Ready."

I held my breath as she clicked the "publish" button.

"And . . . we're live!"

"Congratulations, you two." Sophie peered over my shoulder at the screen. "If you need any wait staff, my roommate is always looking for some extra cash."

I looked up at her. "Does she have waitressing experience?"

"*He* does. And he's cute, too," she added with a wink. "He's putting himself through med school. Gone back after a few years in the workforce."

"Is he single? How old is he?"

I knew exactly where Paige was going with this.

"He's single, and I don't know. Thirty or something? Old."

I chuckled. I remembered when I thought thirty was old, too. That ship had sailed.

"Thirty-something, single, smart, *and* cute?" Paige shot me a meaningful look.

"Paige," I warned.

My mind instantly darted to Ryan. He was thirty-something, single, smart, and cute. And a total hot mess.

"Bailey, we'll need wait staff," Paige said. I shrugged in response. She was right, and a bit of eye candy couldn't hurt for us old, single types. Well, old according to Sophie, anyway.

"Can you flick me his number?" Paige asked.

She slipped her phone out of her jeans pocket and tapped on the screen. "Done. His name is Jason Christie. See you ladies tomorrow." She flashed us a grin as she collected her purse from the back of the kitchen.

"Cute name," Paige lead.

I let out a sigh. "No way."

"What? You signed up to the pact, and the speed dating thing didn't work out."

The memory of the men I'd met that evening had me shuddering. "Definitely not."

"So, you need to put yourself out there."

"Paige, as much as I love you, I don't think 'putting myself out there' with an employee is a great way to go. No matter how cute he *allegedly* is."

"I guess there is that. But we're not giving up on this, you know."

I shrugged. "Okay." Although I *would* like a change of subject. "Now, how about we work out a few options for the wedding and then call it a night?"

Thinking about someone else's happily ever after was preferable to thinking about my own lack of one. And I hoped throwing myself into a new business venture would be just the distraction I needed.

Chapter 9

THE WHOLE NEXT WEEK was business as usual at the café, and coming up with new and fun ideas for Cassie and Will's wedding. They had given us a few guidelines on their tastes, with one thing we had to supply—gourmet burgers. Apparently, they'd bonded for the first time over the "best burgers in town" at a diner and they wanted to remember that on their big day.

Yeah, I know. Cute and romantic, right?

I grabbed a few minutes after the lunch rush to catch up on invoices and noticed an email inquiry via our website, asking us to quote for an upcoming event. It was only small, catering lunch for twelve at a meeting of a company board. But it was our first client—well, the first one we didn't know personally, anyway.

I smiled to myself. Maybe this catering idea was just what I needed to take my mind off my lack of a Last First Date?

I jumped up from my seat at the kitchen counter, almost knocking Paige sideways in the process.

"Whoa!" With impressive dexterity, she managed to keep a tray of frittatas and paninis balanced in her hands.

"Sorry, sorry," I said hastily. "Look!" I pointed at the screen, pressing my lips together to avoid squealing like an excited kid on Christmas morning.

Paige put her tray down on the counter and peered at the screen. She straightened up and looked at me, her hand over her mouth. "Oh, my God!"

"I know, right?"

I'm not proud, but we did actually hop up and down on the spot, clutching hands.

Sophie walked into the kitchen carrying a stack of used dishes. "What's going on, you two?"

"We just got our first catering enquiry," I told her, beaming.

"Cool." She placed the stack of dishes on the counter. "Guess you'd better call my sexy roommate Jason, then." She shot me a look I chose to ignore.

I mean, why was it when you were single everyone wanted to match-make you? As if you couldn't be happy unless you were in a relationship?

Forget the fact I'd agreed to a pact to marry the next guy I dated and *did* want to find my special someone. This was on principle.

"We *might* need to win their business first before we go hiring anyone new," I replied.

"Well, when you do, let me know." Sophie left the kitchen, heading back out to serve a customer.

"I'll email them back, ask them what they're looking for, and send them some sample menus." I sat back down at my laptop to compose a winning email.

"Sounds great. Oh, I knew this would work."

As I began to type, I smiled to myself. I hoped she was right.

LATER THAT DAY, I was working alongside Sophie at the counter serving the last lunch customers when Ryan sauntered across the café floor. He hadn't come at his usual time again this morning, and I'd assumed it just wasn't a day for the Norse gods to visit us mere mortals.

Either that or he was just as confused by what had almost happened as I was.

I mumbled my hello and tried not to notice the way his white shirt showed off his light tan, or the fact he shot me an electric look with those eyes of his when he said hello.

"Hi, Ryan," Sophie cooed beside me.

"Hey, Soph. Looking good today." He smiled at Sophie and then looked back at me. "You too, Bailey."

Don't blush, don't blush, don't blush.

I blushed.

Man, I was so freaking predictable.

"Are you after a coffee?" Sophie asked as I scanned the counter for something to cool my burning cheeks. AC? An iceberg, perhaps?

I found nothing.

"Sure am."

"Your usual? Or did you want to try something new?"

"My usual would be great, thanks."

Knowing my face was probably the color of a ripe tomato about now, I excused myself, turned, and walked into the kitchen. I placed my palms on the cool counter then lifted them to my face, hoping they would counter the heat.

What was it about this guy that made me constantly react like a teenager with a crush?

"You okay?" Paige's voice startled me. "You look all hot and bothered."

"Oh, yes. Fine, thanks."

She narrowed her eyes at me, unconvinced. "Something's got you worked up."

"What? Oh, nothing. It's just a hot flash or something. Weird, right?"

What? I was menopausal now?

"A hot flash?"

Before I could stop her, she shot past me and out into the café.

I scrunched my eyes shut. Only Ryan and Sophie were at the counter when I came in here. It wouldn't exactly take a rocket scientist to put two and two together and work out "Bailey's got a crush on Ryan."

I moved further into the kitchen, searching for something to do to take my mind off what was coming, when Paige came back in. My secret crush would be outed, and she'd make it her personal mission to match-make Ryan and me.

This was not going to be pretty.

I began to rinse the stack of lunchtime dishes, placing them in the industrial dishwasher. It didn't take long before Paige was standing beside me.

"There are two possibilities here—you either like an elderly gentleman with a walking stick and a cravat who just walked in, or someone else."

"Who said I liked anyone?" I bluffed.

"Blushing usually equals attraction. And you're far too young for the menopause, no matter what you claim."

"Maybe I'm coming down with something. Have you thought of that?"

Yeah, I heard it. I was getting desperate now. I'd be talking about contracting Bubonic Plague in a moment.

Paige shook her head. "No. You're not sick. You like someone. You like Ryan Jones."

She'd hit the hot nail on the head. There was clearly no beating about the bush.

I turned to look at her. "No. Yes." I let out an exasperated puff of air. "I don't want to."

A smile teased at the edges of her mouth. "But you do."

I bit my lip and nodded. I'd never been a good liar. Now wasn't the time to try to improve my lack of skill in that department.

Paige's pretty face broke into a broad grin, and she placed her hand over her heart. "Oh, my gosh. You would be such a gorgeous couple! You with your dark hair and olive skin, and him with that blonde Northern European thing he's got going on."

I wagged my finger at her. "No, Paige. No matchmaking. It's just a silly crush because he's all cute and Thor-like."

"Thor-like?"

"You know, the superhero guy with the hammer?"

"Ah, Chris Hemsworth." She nodded, her eyes sparkling. "Yeah, I can totally see that."

"And anyway, he's not interested in me."

Her eyebrows hit her hairline. "He's not?"

I shook my head. "No. He's all bitter and twisted about his ex. You know that. He made it really clear he's not looking for anything when he was over at my place last—" Too late, I stopped myself from finishing my sentence.

The cat was well and truly out of the bag, prowling around the room.

Paige's eyes widened. "He was at your *house*?"

"Don't make a big deal about it, 'kay? He was just in the neighborhood and dropped in to say hi. That's all."

"Ryan Jones just happened to be in your neighborhood, huh?" Her eyes danced.

"No, Paige. Don't."

"What?" She was acting all innocent now. "It's just interesting to me, that's all. I mean, he doesn't live anywhere near you, and he went to the effort to drop by when you were home?"

Well, when she put it like that . . . *No*. I wasn't going to make something out of nothing.

"He's moved, actually. He lives on Dorchester Street."

"Does he, now?" She tapped her finger to her chin. "Well, isn't that convenient?"

"Bailey? Paige?" Sophie called from the café.

"I'll take over here. You go out into the café, *and* Ryan." Paige took a dirty plate from my hand and placed it in the dishwasher. "And we'll talk about this later."

I knew exactly what she was doing.

And part of me liked it, despite the fact she would be relentless with her matchmaking from now on.

"Go on. Sophie needs you."

I let out a puff of air, shooting Paige a look.

This was going to be excruciating.

I walked through the kitchen and out into the café where a

couple of women were perusing the cabinet food at the counter. Sophie was working at the coffee machine, and Ryan was standing beside the register. His eyes flashed to mine, and he shot me a smile before he looked away.

"How may I help you?" I concentrated on the women at the cabinet—and definitely not on Ryan.

"Which one of these cakes can you recommend?" a woman with bright purple hair asked. Her hair was possibly not altogether natural.

"I've heard they're all good. This place is famous for its cakes, right?" The second woman raised her brows at me.

"We do enjoy our cake here, that's true." I smiled at them. "As for what I can recommend, it depends on what you like. The carrot cake with cream cheese frosting is super moist, and we like to think it's a little healthy, due to the carrots." I shot her a smile as I pointed at the next cake. "Then there's the chocolate and raspberry cake. It's gluten-free, if you're into that. Most importantly though, it's totally delicious."

"That sounds good," said Purple Hair.

"What's that one?" the other woman said, pointing at another cake.

"That's *Cassata alla Siciliana*," Ryan said to the women in slightly butchered Italian before I had the chance to respond. "It's like an Italian cheesecake. Try it, you'll love it."

"Sold," Purple Hair said to Ryan. "I'll have a slice of that, please."

"Me too," her friend added.

I took their coffee order, they paid, and I told them I'd bring their food and drinks over to them once it was ready.

"Here you are, Ryan." Sophie handed him his coffee. I noticed it was in a takeout cup.

My heart sank.

"I hope you didn't mind me jumping in there," he said to me.

"No, no. It's fine. Thank you, in fact."

"For what?"

Good question.

"Selling the cake, I guess?"

Ryan shrugged, smiling. "All I know is they taste great."

"Thanks," Sophie and I both said in unison.

I shot her a sideways look. Geez, it was like we were the Ryan Jones fangirl club over here.

"Well, I gotta go. Thanks for the coffee, Soph."

"Any time," she cooed.

He glanced at me, raising his chin. "See you 'round, Bailey."

"See you 'round," I echoed. I watched as he walked out of the café and onto the street, trying not to notice how cute he looked as he walked away.

I let out a sigh. I guess that was just another weird exchange in the Ryan-Bailey show.

"Tell me about your pact." Sophie interrupted my reverie.

"My what?"

"You know, the thing where you and Paige and the other girls all agreed to date men or something?"

"Oh, the Last First Date pact."

"That's the one."

"Well, it's designed to do what it says on the can—you marry the next guy you go on a date with."

"Talk about putting the pressure on!"

"Yeah. I guess."

If you could find someone you wanted to date in the first place, that was. Or, more appropriately, if you could find someone who wasn't still messed up over their ex and actually kissed you while standing on your doorstep instead of just looking like he wanted to.

But maybe I was being too specific.

"Can anyone join?" Sophie asked.

"I guess. I didn't make up the rules. I think you'd need to talk to Cassie, or maybe Paige?" I focused my attention on rearranging the cabinet food.

Sophie nodded, a smile forming on her face. "I might do that. I think I know who I might choose, too."

I snapped my head in her direction. She had a cloth in hand and had set about cleaning the coffee machine.

I watched her, thinking. Would she choose Ryan? She certainly seemed to get a little, I don't know, "girly" when he was here. I pressed my lips together.

Hmm. A lot like me.

My eyes drifted out the window to the people walking by. I wondered if I'd ever know why Ryan visited me at home that day—and whether he was actually going to kiss me.

Or, much likelier, if it had all been a figment of my overactive imagination.

Chapter 10

"WOW, GIRLS. THIS LOOKS amazing!" Cassie's eyes welled up with tears.

Paige, Cassie, Will, and I were sitting at a table in the closed café. Paige and I had just finished presenting our catering ideas to Cassie and Will for their wedding, and Cassie quite clearly liked what we had suggested. Will simply smiled at us.

"So, you like it?" Paige asked.

"Like it? I *love* it." She leant over the table and collected Paige in a watery hug before turning her attention to me.

"This is going to be such a beautiful wedding," I said into her thick auburn hair.

"I won't get all emotional and hug you, because, you know, I'm a guy. But thanks," Will said with his cheeky grin.

When Cassie pulled away, her tears had spilled over. Paige offered her a tissue, which she accepted, muttering her thanks as she sat back down at the table next to her fiancé.

She turned to Will. "What do you think?"

"Burgers and fries? Total man-feast. Who knew I could get a girl to agree to that for our wedding?" He wrapped his arm around her shoulder and pulled her into him.

"It's more than just burgers and fries, you know," Cassie said.

"Okay, *fancy* burgers and fries. Better?"

Cassie laughed, shaking her head and rolling her eyes. "Men."

"What?" Will protested.

It was true. They'd opted for burgers and fries for the main meal, but they weren't your everyday, run of the mill variety. No way. We were doing grass-fed beef burgers with aioli, beet relish, and arugula on a ciabatta bun. The fries were garlic sweet potato and parsnip.

See? Fancy.

"So, the dinner is exactly what we want. What about the cake?" Cassie asked.

"Well, I have some ideas on that front." I turned Paige's laptop around and searched through the files until I found the document I'd prepared earlier. I pulled the file up and swung the laptop back so it was facing the happy couple. "What do you think?" I beamed at them, hoping they'd think my idea was the stroke of genius I did.

After all, if there was one thing I knew in this life, it was cake.

Men? Not so much.

I watched their faces in expectation as they studied the image on the screen. Will's face broke into a broad grin.

Cassie's did not.

Her eyes darted from the image to Will and then to me.

"What is it, Cassie? You don't like it?"

"I'm not sure."

"Well, I do." Will leaned back in his chair. "What's not to like?"

"Cassie?" I raised my brows.

"I don't know, Bailey." She shrugged. "The fruit flavor will be amazing, exactly what we wanted, but the shape of it? I guess it doesn't feel very wedding-y, you know? I mean, it's a *golf ball*."

"Exactly. Like the way Will proposed to you at the golf driving range," Paige said. "You know, with the ring in the golf ball. We thought it would be totally cute."

Cassie shrugged. "I appreciate the thought, but I think I'd like something more traditional. Tiered, maybe?"

I guessed we'd missed the mark.

"We can do that, right, Bailey?" Paige said.

"No problem. Tiered it is. If you're not incredibly happy, then we're not doing our job right." I glanced at Paige.

Cassie nodded, the tension disappearing from her features.

"All right. We're on it," I said.

"Well, we'd better get going." Cassie pushed her chair out from the table.

"Are you coming to the Cozy Cottage Jam later?" Paige asked.

"Actually, we're going to be a little late for it this week. We're meeting up with the owners of The Windsor Inn." Cassie's face glowed.

The Windsor Inn was an old home that had been made into a gorgeous wedding venue. I'd been to a couple of weddings there myself over the years and loved the way they held the weddings outside under a wisteria-lined pergola in an English country garden, complete with a pond and a little bridge. It was very romantic.

"Such a nice spot, you two," Paige said.

"I know, right? We're excited."

"Well, you are. I'm still thinking about the burgers and fries," Will added.

I walked over to the front door, unbolted it, and let Cassie and Will out. "Have a great evening. We'll get some more cake designs to you early next week."

"I know you'll do an amazing job." Cassie gave me a hug goodbye.

After the golf ball cake disaster, I wasn't so sure.

"Let's stick with traditional," I said as Paige and I waved them goodbye and locked the door.

"I was sure they would go for the golf ball."

"Well, one of them did."

"Right. I suppose we'd better set up for the Jam night." Paige walked around the counter toward the kitchen. "Unless you have a hot date with He Who Shall Not Be Named."

I rolled my eyes. "No, I don't."

"Really? I was sure he was going to ask you out."

I shook my head as I followed her into the kitchen. I opened the refrigerator and began to collect ingredients. "Paige, all that happened was he dropped by my house one day after work. We had a drink, he left. End of story."

Although Ryan had been in the café a handful of times since then, he'd been nothing but pleasant and chatty.

"And anyway, he hasn't been here much lately. He's clearly not interested in me."

"But the fact he dropped by your place, totally out of the blue like that, *has* to mean something."

With ingredients in my arms, I closed the door behind me with my foot. "Yes, it does mean something. It means he was in my neighborhood so dropped by."

She shook her head, her eyes dancing. "He's going to ask you out. I just know it."

I placed my items on the counter and turned to face her. "Paige!" I was getting sick of this now.

She put her hands up in the surrender sign. "All right. I'll drop it. But if he doesn't ask you out soon, I'll be surprised. I've seen the way he looks at you. That's all I'm saying."

FRIDAY NIGHT JAMS at the Cozy Cottage were a lot of fun—and a *lot* of work. We were fully booked most Fridays these days, and we needed to get extra staff in to help out. We served basic meals, such as toasted sandwiches or lasagna and salads, and we'd got our license to serve beer and wine. Although I had to admit, sometimes I cursed it when tone deaf singers got Dutch courage from one too many on our open mic nights. #Screechingcats

Luckily, tonight was not an open mic night. Instead, we'd gotten a local act we'd had once or twice before, a folk singer whose music was gentle and melodic. Just what I needed after a long week.

I was behind the counter serving a customer when Marissa and Cassie turned up, excited looks on their faces.

"Thank you so much. We'll bring that over to you when it's ready." I handed the customer his receipt and a number in a metal holder shaped like a cupcake on top of a pole. Very appropriate for our cake-focused café.

I turned my friends. "What has you two so amped?"

"Remember that guy from the speed dating? The one with the flicky hair?" Cassie asked.

"He thought he was God's gift to women," Marissa added with a roll of her eyes.

"Oh, you mean Fake Jamie, the guy who claimed he was famous in England."

"That's the one," Cassie said.

"What about him?" Fake Jamie hadn't entered my mind since the evening of the speed dating disaster. Which was exactly the way I liked it.

"He's here," they both said in unison.

"Here? Well, that's fine." I scanned the room, looking for a guy who looked like a Bee Gees wannabe. I spotted him at one of the tables, talking with a redhead, looking just the way he had the evening of the speed dating—too smooth, very impressed with himself.

Guys like him left me cold.

"But, *ugh*." Marissa pulled a face.

I laughed. "It is a free country, you know."

"The question is *why* is he here? Did you tell him this was your café?" Cassie was concerned.

I thought back to our four-minute "date" and all I could recall was his sleazy lines and his claim he was too famous to find love. "I don't think so. But really, it's fine. He moved on to that blonde woman at the next table. He'd have completely forgotten about me within about two seconds flat."

Cassie shrugged. "Maybe."

The evening progressed as it usually did, with me, Paige, Sophie, and a couple of our part-time workers run off our feet. The place was packed, and people seemed to be having a good time.

Cassie and Will were on a double date with Marissa and Nash, sitting at a table near the counter. I was pouring out a couple of glasses of Pinot Gris when I noticed Josh walk through the door. I smiled at him and he smiled back.

I corked the wine bottle and put it back in the wine refrigerator we'd had installed under the counter. When I looked back up, Josh had pulled a chair up at Cassie and Marissa's table and there was another man standing next to him, with his back to me.

I tried to play it down, but my heart rate kicked up a notch at the sight of him.

It was Ryan.

As if sensing my eyes on him, he turned and shot me a smile, raising his chin the way guys do. I smiled back at him, willing my heart to return to normal.

As I said, Ryan Jones is bad for my cardiac health.

"Err, how much is that?" the woman I had been serving asked.

I dragged my eyes from Ryan back to her. "Oh, sorry. I got distracted. That's twenty-three dollars, please."

She handed over her credit card, and I completed the transaction. After she'd gone, I stole another glance at Ryan. He was now sitting down, sandwiched between his sister and Josh.

Paige nudged my arm, nodding in his direction. "Tonight could be the night, you know. He's looking super cute, don't you think?"

I shook my head, ignoring her comment. Really, it was time she moved on, just like Ryan had. If in fact he'd had anything to move on from.

"I'll be right back." I walked around the counter, past a handful of tables, and out through the door that led down a hallway to the bathrooms. With the door back into the café closed, I leant up against the wall and closed my eyes. I needed a breather, and this was as good a place as any.

Within about ten seconds, the door from the café swung open and the hallway was instantly filled with music. I opened my eyes to see Fake Jamie walking toward me.

I pushed myself off the wall to face him.

"Hello, babe," he said in his thick accent.

"Hi." I forced smile. I wasn't his "babe," but he was a paying customer tonight, so I wasn't going to point it out. "Are you having a fun evening?"

"Yeah. Top place you got here."

"Thanks."

"I, ah, I looked for you, the other night. At the speed dating thing." He put his hand on the wall beside me. He was a big, solid guy, and took up most of the width of the hallway.

I began to feel uncomfortable. "Oh, yes. I had to go. Did you . . . did you get any second dates?"

I really didn't want to know the answer. I just wanted to get back to the café.

"Not from the lady I wanted one from." He moved his body closer to mine.

I caught a whiff of his cologne as I took a step back, banging up against the wall. I was well and truly cornered—and I didn't like it one little bit.

"That was you, babe, in case you were wondering."

"Okay, yes, gotcha. I guess we didn't get that connection they went on about that night, right?" I cleared my throat, pushing down my rising panic. "Anyway, if you'll excuse me, I have customers to serve."

He ran his fingers through his hair, fixing me with his gaze. I think it was meant to be sexy.

It wasn't.

"I feel a pretty strong connection to you right now, Cointreau."

I chewed my lip. I remembered he thought I was named after a bottle of alcohol. I didn't bother to correct him.

"Well, I'm sorry, but I don't. And I need to get back to my café. So, if you wouldn't mind?" I eyed his hand, pressed against the wall above my shoulder.

He leant in closer to me. I could smell the garlic on his breath. "How about a little kiss before you go, then?"

"No thank you."

He reached up with his free hand and touched my face.

I recoiled from him, barely believing what was happening. "I said no."

And then I saw red.

In a flash of anger, I pushed him out of the way, the element of surprise working in my favor. I rushed down the hallway, only for him to grab me by the arm. I whipped my head to look at him. "Let me go."

The door swung open toward us, the music pouring into the narrow hallway once more. I snapped my head to see who it was, and looked up into Ryan's face.

His eyes darted from me to Fake Jamie and back again. "Everything okay here?" Concern was written across his handsome face.

I looked back at Fake Jamie and tugged my arm away from him with force. "I was just leaving." Despite my shaking limbs, I shot Fake Jamie a pointed "don't mess with me" look.

"Yeah, me too, mate," he spat. "You're welcome to her." Fake Jamie pushed past me. "Frigid bitch."

My jaw dropped as he let the door swing closed behind him. I let out a sigh of relief, slumping against the wall.

"You sure you're okay?" Ryan asked, his voice only just loud enough to be heard over the music.

I nodded, biting my lip, not trusting my voice to speak. To my utter mortification, tears stung my eyes.

"You're not okay."

"No, I am. He was just persistent, that's all." I could still feel the tight grip of his hand on my arm, smell his cologne, the garlic on his breath. I rubbed my arm, taking a few deep breaths to calm my nerves.

"And you didn't want him to be persistent, right? I mean, you don't like that guy?"

My eyes bulged. "No!"

A shadow moved across his face, his jaw locked. "Got it."

He turned on his heel, swung the door open, and stomped across the café floor. I followed, pausing in the doorway. Ryan reached Fake Jamie's table where he had already sat down with his date. From my position, I could tell words were being exchanged, Fake Jamie standing up to face Ryan, an angry scowl on his face.

As much as it felt pretty darn amazing to have my honor

defended by Ryan, I rushed over to them. The last thing we wanted was a couple of guys squaring off for a fight in the café. Not good for business.

By the time I got there, Fake Jamie had his hands up in the surrender sign, Ryan glaring at him, his hands clenched at his sides.

Thor? *Oh, yes.*

"All right, mate. Keep your hair on." Fake Jamie turned to his date. "Come on, darling'. We're leaving." He shot me a look meant to wither. "This place sucks."

Ryan stood back as Fake Jamie led his confused girlfriend past us and out the door. Once they were gone, he turned to me and shook his head. "What a jerk."

I smiled back. I could think of quite a few other names to call him right now. Jerk was just the tip of the iceberg.

"Thanks for . . . you know." What? *Rescuing me like a damsel in distress?*

I'd never gone in for that sort of thing, but I had to admit, Ryan dealing with Fake Jamie in that way had felt good.

And, if he hadn't turned up when he had, I'm not sure how things would have turned out.

"Did you know that guy?"

"I met him at the speed dating thing."

"Well, I think that's the last you're going to see of him."

I looked out the window to the darkened street outside, illuminated in patches by streetlights.

After the scare I'd just had, I hoped he was right.

Chapter 11

I SAT AT THE kitchen counter, a half empty glass of wine in my hand. Although the evening was winding down and customers had begun to leave, I knew I still had work to do. But Ryan had insisted I sit down with a drink to calm my nerves.

And it was a good plan. The alcohol had warmed my belly, the memory of Fake Jamie's unwanted advances fading.

Ryan sat beside me, disquiet written across his face.

"You don't have to sit here with me, you know. I'm feeling a whole lot better now. And I have loads to do."

"Paige is on it. She told me to stay with you."

I did an internal eye roll. Any chance she could get to throw us together. "I'm sure she did." A smile teased at the edges of my mouth.

"What?" Ryan asked.

I shook my head. "Nothing. Just Paige being Paige."

"Well, it's good to see that smile back on your beautiful face."

I blinked at him. First, he got all manly kicking Fake Jamie out on his butt, now he was calling me beautiful?

Wow, a girl could really fall for a guy like Ryan.

"OMG! Paige just told us what happened!" Marissa came

bustling into the kitchen, Cassie, Nash, Will, and Josh hot on her heels.

Did *everyone* know about this now?

"I'm fine, really," I protested, though it was clear no one believed me.

Marissa and Cassie fussed over me, Cassie refilling my glass with more wine, and Marissa patting me on the back like I was a baby with wind.

"Heard you stood up for her," Nash said to Ryan. "Tossed the guy out on his ear."

Ryan shrugged. "You'd have done the same."

"Good work, man." Will slapped Ryan on the back.

"I can't believe it was that sleazy guy from the speed dating," Marissa said. "I feel so bad I sent you on that."

"Hey, do you think he came here on purpose? You know, to find Bailey?" Josh said.

"Oh, my gosh. Maybe he did!" Cassie's eyes wide.

"All right, you guys." I stood up. "Before you develop any stalker conspiracy theories and get me completely drunk—" I eyed the fresh wine bottle in Cassie's hand. "He didn't even remember my name. It was just an unfortunate coincidence that he came here tonight and did what he did. Nothing more."

"You need a bouncer. A big, gnarly looking one who can scare idiots like that guy off," Nash said to agreement from the men and women alike.

"I think she should call the police," Marissa said.

"Enough!" Everyone stopped and gaped at me. "No bouncers, no police. I'm fine. And now I have a café to clean up and prepare for opening tomorrow. And you all have homes to go to."

"We're just trying to help," Cassie said.

"I know you are. And to help me right now, you can all go home."

They muttered and hung their heads like a group of naughty school children being sent off for punishment.

Paige came into the kitchen, a tray of empty dishes in her

hands. "What are you all doing in here?" She placed the tray on the counter. "Right, off you go. Shoo! Shoo!"

I smiled to myself as I watched her bustle everyone out of the kitchen. I went to take a sip of my wine, thought better of it, and poured the glass down the sink. I had a café to prepare for tomorrow and an early morning ahead of me. I needed a clear head.

Paige came back into the kitchen, and we set about organizing and cleaning up. Sophie was stacking the chairs onto the tables in the café, and Penny, one of our casual employees, was busy sweeping. They were almost done.

"Can I help?" Ryan asked, appearing in the doorway.

"You've done enough already," I said with a smile.

He shook his head. "Give me something to do." He clearly wasn't taking no for an answer.

"All right." I handed him a cloth and a bottle of disinfectant. "Counter tops, please."

He flashed me his smile and went to work.

I tried not to watch him as he sprayed and wiped, a knot forming in my belly at how sweet he was being to me. I may well have been able to get away from Fake Jamie in the hallway on my own, but Ryan had turned up at just the right time. And now he was here, watching out for me.

Really, it was enough to make a girl swoon.

Which I was *not* going to let myself do.

As wonderful as he'd been to me tonight, I knew he was totally anti-love. Otherwise something might have already happened between us.

Wouldn't it?

We worked for the best part of an hour, until my feet ached, and all I could think of was soaking in a warm tub and forgetting about the evening.

With her jacket already on, Paige breezed past me. "I'm off. See you tomorrow." Without waiting for a reply, she swung the back door open where Josh was waiting for her. "Come on, you two."

Penny and Sophie, also in their jackets, their purses slung over their shoulders, slunk past. Sophie paused to talk with Ryan, and I noticed Paige flashed her a look. "I said, come on, Sophie."

Sophie let out a frustrated puff of air. "All right." She looked up at Ryan, towering above her diminutive frame. "See you next time, Ryan."

"See you, Soph."

Both the girls called out, "Bye, Bailey," and Paige pulled the door behind them, giving me a quick wink.

And then it was just Ryan and me.

Paige could not have been any less subtle if she'd paraded around the kitchen with a large neon sign that read "we are now leaving Ryan and Bailey alone together."

I glanced at Ryan. He was standing with his hands stuffed into his jeans pockets, looking about as uncomfortable as I felt.

"Well, thanks a lot for helping. You really didn't need to."

"I wanted to. I . . . I want to make sure you get home all right, too."

I let out a laugh. "I've been doing it on my own for a long time now."

"You know what I mean. That jerk might still be lurking around out there."

I shuddered at the thought.

"My car is just across the street. Let me see you home?" His tone was uncompromising.

It made me feel . . . safe. I didn't know what it was about Ryan—besides his obvious hotness, that was—but I felt protected around him, secure.

I liked it.

I opened my mouth to protest, decided against it. "Sure, that would be great."

I gave the café a last check over and collected my things. I locked the door behind us, and Ryan and I crossed the street to his car.

No Fake Jamie in sight.

"How's the new place?" I buckled up in the front seat of his SUV.

"It's great, actually. I forgot how much I like to live on my own. My furniture, my mess, my moldy cheese in the refrigerator."

"Eww, that does not sound good."

He laughed as he turned the ignition over and pulled out into the quiet street. "After sleeping on Marissa's sofa for way too long, I'm happy to let my cheese go green in my own refrigerator."

We chatted about all sorts of things, from the rise in rents to hair product and a bunch of things between. I laughed and enjoyed myself, the unsavory event of the night slipping from my mind.

After what felt like only a matter of seconds, he pulled his car into my driveway and put it in park.

"Thanks for the ride," I said, unbuckling my seatbelt.

"I'll see you inside."

I knew there was no point trying to argue. Ryan Jones was a man who had made up his mind. I wasn't about to stand in his way.

And, if I were totally honest, I kinda hoped his desire to protect me came from a desire *for* me.

Yup, I still hadn't let that hope go.

I tried to ignore the butterflies in my belly as I slipped out of the car. I pulled my keys from my purse, and Ryan and I walked to my front door.

"Did you want to come in for a drink?" I offered, *hoping, hoping, hoping* . . .

"Sure. That sounds good."

I beamed at him. A small voice in the back of my head said *he likes you, Paige is right.* I was finding it hard to ignore.

Once inside, I slipped my jacket off and hung it up. Although I would have loved nothing more than to peel my shoes off and pad around in bare feet, I didn't. I wanted to look cute for Ryan, and if that meant a few more moments of shoe-inflicted torture, so be it.

"Beer?" I asked over my shoulder as I walked to my kitchen.

"What? No milk this time?"

I let out a laugh as I pulled a couple of cold ones out of the refrigerator. I opened them up and carried them to the living room where Ryan was examining my photos—just like he had the last time he was here.

"I see you went for the cap-free variety tonight," he said as I handed him his bottle.

I laughed. "My dentist will be disappointed. No expensive work for me."

We both took sips of our beer, and I suggested we take a seat. I sat down on the sofa, and this time, he sat down next to me.

I tried not to read anything into it.

I failed.

Big time.

"So, those Cozy Cottage Jam things are popular, huh?"

"They are." Thanks to them, Friday had become our biggest grossing day of the week. "You should sing some time, at the open mic night. We've got one coming up soon."

He laughed, almost spraying his beer. "Have you heard me sing?"

"No."

"And there's a very good reason for that."

"I figured you could sing. Marissa's good." I remembered how she had sung a love song at the open mic night that had won Nash's heart a few months back.

He shook his head "Nope. I didn't get that gene."

"Shame. Women love a guy who can sing."

Was I flirting? Yup, I think I was.

"I can do other things, you know."

"Oh yeah? Like what?"

"I'm a pretty handy tennis player, and I'm pretty sure I could whip your butt in a game of Wii Baseball."

I raised my eyebrows. "Is that so?" I stood up and stepped over to the TV cabinet. I pulled out a couple of white remote controls, turned to face him, holding one in each hand. "I happen to be quite a good tennis player myself, and I can almost guarantee I could whip *your* butt on Wii." I waggled the remotes in the air.

"You've got a Wii console?"

I nodded, grinning. "Mm-hm."

"Wow, that's so retro of you."

I shrugged. "Does ten years ago actually count as 'retro?'"

He laughed. It was low and rumbled through me, making me smile. "Sure, it does. Now hand one of those over, De Luca."

I passed him one of the remotes, trying not to smile at his use of my last name. "Let's see who can whip whose butt, shall we?"

Yup, definitely flirting now. And I was enjoying it. A lot.

I switched on the TV and powered up the console, selecting "baseball" for two players.

"Choose your team, Jones."

Two could play at the last name game.

We set about choosing which Mii characters we wanted in our respective teams and then I was up, batting first. As was my custom, I stood up to make my hit, getting into the correct posture I'd seen players do on TV.

"Do you do that every time?" Ryan asked from his position on the sofa, amusement written across his face.

"Be quiet. I'm concentrating."

Ryan laughed then pitched the ball. I swiped at it, missing it completely.

"Oh, too bad," he teased.

"I'm just warming up." I readied myself again. This time when he pitched I whacked the ball and got a home run. I grinned at him. "And that, Mr. Jones, is how you do it."

He shook his head, smiling.

We cycled through my players until I had a decent score on the board—not my personal best, but then I hadn't played Wii for a long time.

Not since Dan.

The thought of him made me stop in my tracks. This Wii console was his, and he'd brought it over here when we'd started to get serious. I remembered the fun evenings we'd had together playing this game, of how we'd pretended not to be competitive with one another while we so were. I'd never played any video game before we started dating, and Dan taught me how.

"You didn't even take a swing at that." Ryan's voice interrupted my walk down memory lane.

"Momentary lapse of concentration. I'm back on it."

My innings over, I prepared myself to pitch. Again, Ryan laughed when I did a couple of practice runs, lifting my left leg and holding the remote in my hand like a ball in a mitt.

"What?" I mock-glared at him, pretending I was offended.

"I don't know. You look so pretty in that dress, and then you pitch like you mean it."

"I totally mean it. Now bring it."

We played and bantered with one another until eventually I won the match in the final seconds. It was a real edge-of-your-seat kinda finish to the game.

I'd love to say I was modest about my victory. I was not. I danced around my living room, butchering Queen's famous song with "*I* am the champion" while Ryan watched on, laughing.

Once I'd finished, he stood up and extended his hand. "Well done, De Luca. A match well played."

I took his hand in mine and shook it. "Well played to you, too. You put up a good fight."

"We'll have to have a rematch someday soon."

There was something in the way he said "someday soon" that had my tummy doing a flip. Neither of us let go of the other's hand and as we stood together, something shifted between us.

Gone was the lively banter, the fun between friends.

"Bailey, I . . . I didn't like that guy treating you the way he did."

I pressed my lips together. "Me neither."

"It did something to me."

"What did it do . . . exactly?" I held my breath, hope rising in me like yeast in bread.

"I don't know. It was like it forced me to wake up. Does that make sense?"

I opened my mouth to speak. *Wake up from what?* I knew what he wanted to be waking up from, but I didn't say anything. Instead, I shook my head.

He let out a puff of air, our hands still linked. "The way he had a hold of your arm, the way it was obvious what he intended to do to you? Well, it sure made see red. I couldn't stand by and watch it."

He shrugged. "I know it makes me seem like I think I'm some kind of hero."

Thor, maybe?

"No, you did the right thing. He'd overstepped the line. Thank you."

"It . . . it did something else to me, too."

"What?" My voice came out breathless.

"It made me realize what an idiot I've been."

I bit my lip. "You've been an idiot?"

He let out a small laugh. "Yeah. You're this great girl and I've been . . . well, I've been thinking about you a lot." He glanced from my eyes to my lips and back again.

I held my breath.

"Actually, I've wanted to kiss you for a long time. Since the day we met, in fact."

My eyes got huge. "You have? But that was ages ago." I thought of how I'd had an instant attraction to him the first time I saw him, too. It was at the Cozy Cottage, all that time ago.

He nodded, moving his free hand to my shoulder. "See? Idiot."

Suddenly nervous, the relaxed camaraderie of the last hour had morphed into something else. I looked up into his eyes, my heart pounding in my chest. In a beat, we moved closer to one another so we were mere inches apart. He bent his head down toward me, and I tilted mine up to meet him, closing my eyes. He brushed his lips gently against mine.

It was brief, electric.

Wonderful.

I opened my eyes as he pulled away.

He cleared his throat. "Sorry, I . . . I shouldn't have done that."

"Why not?" My voice was breathless.

His eyes darted back to mine. They were full of unspoken words. "Because I . . . because I like you. *Really* like you."

I let out a light laugh, giddy with what had just happened between us, with what he was saying. "That's why you can't kiss me?" I shook my head. "Ryan, that has got to be the stupidest thing I think I've ever heard."

His face creased into a smile that had me melting at the knees. "It kinda is, isn't it?"

"Totally."

His eyes flashed. "Want to do it again?"

Is the Pope Catholic?

"Oh, yeah."

This time he crushed his lips against mine, his fingers tangled up in my curls, my body tingling from the top of my head to my toes. I breathed in his scent, lost in the kiss, lost in his embrace.

And it was a good kiss, the kind that made your toes curl, the kind that left you breathless, alive. There were fireworks and stars and electricity bouncing off the walls.

It was the kind of kiss you wanted to go on forever. The kind you never forget.

Chapter 12

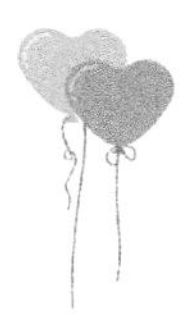

THE FOLLOWING DAY, I swear I could have floated into the café on a cloud. I was light and ecstatically happy. I couldn't stop grinning. I'd had to pinch myself when I woke up with my alarm, tell myself it wasn't all a dream.

Ryan had professed his feelings to me. He liked me just as much as I like him, since the day we met, in fact, but wasn't ready for anything new following his break-up.

And not only that, we'd kissed—and kissed and kissed.

It was . . . *heavenly*.

I walked passed Addi's empty florist shop, a "for lease" sign pasted to the window. I wondered who would take the place on, what sort of business we'd have next to the café. Whoever it was, I hope they did it soon. There was something about this place, something I couldn't quite put my finger on.

I guess it needed someone to love it.

I let out a contented sigh as I unlocked the door, floated to the kitchen where I flicked on the lights, and stowed my purse away. I was the first one in most mornings, and I was thankful for it today. It gave me the chance to stay in my Ryan happiness bubble for just that little bit longer before it got hijacked by the busy café.

Switching on the oven, I got to work. Saturdays had become one of our busiest mornings, with brunches and take-outs, people often dropping in with their dogs or kids to get their caffeine fix to go, often a slice of cake, too.

Paige walked through the back door. "Well?" she asked before she'd even closed it behind her.

"Well, good morning." I bit back a smile. I knew she wanted to know if anything had happened with Ryan after she'd left last night.

She plunked her purse down on the counter. "You're not going to hold out on me, are you?"

I couldn't stop my smile from spreading right across my face.

"Oh, my." She placed her hand over her heart. "Something *did* happen, didn't it?"

I nodded, scrunching up my face. "Kinda."

Paige let out one of her characteristic happy squeals. "Tell me everything!"

"Okay." I told her about how we'd played Wii, how we'd had so much fun together, how he'd told me he had feelings for me.

"Well, I could have told you *that*. And?"

"And . . . we might have kissed."

She clapped her hands together. "I knew it! Oh, I'm so happy for you. You two are perfect together."

"I don't know about perfect."

She laughed. "Have you seen yourselves?"

I thought of Ryan with his messy crop of dark blonde hair, trimmed beard, and broad shoulders.

She beamed at me. "When are you seeing him again?"

Last night he'd stood on my doorstep, saying goodnight with another spectacular kiss. Neither of us had wanted the evening to end.

"We didn't make any plans."

"He'll probably turn up with flowers today or something, you watch. Oh, this is so exciting. Think about it. You went to the speed dating thing to meet your Last First Date, and Ryan was there! We all thought it would be one of the guys in the speed dating, but it wasn't."

"True."

"Bailey, don't you see? Ryan is your guy, he's your Last First Date."

I rubbed the back of my neck. Although I really liked Ryan—and kissing him could very easily become my new favorite pastime—I didn't want to get ahead of myself. "I don't know about that. I mean, I like him, but a Last First Date is a big thing."

"Oh, Bailey, you'll see. You so deserve to be with a great guy."

In an instant, my mind darted to another great guy, one I had been lucky enough to be with—Dan. I'd opened up to Paige about him a long time ago, telling her how it had almost destroyed me when he'd died. I'd thought I was going to spend the rest of my life with him, I'd thought *he* was my Last First Date.

My chest tightened at the memory of our first date. If I'm honest, it hadn't exactly gone to plan. In fact, it was kind of a miracle we ended up dating at all. He turned up late, spilled his spaghetti sauce all over his white buttoned shirt, and kept making stupid jokes that weren't even funny. I remember coming home to my cottage that night and deciding, as cute as he was, he wasn't the guy for me.

And then, the next morning, I got a text from him asking me to meet him for a cup of coffee. I figured I'd let him down gently, and it was kinder to do that in person.

He explained he was so nervous on our date he could barely see straight. Nervous because he thought I was so beautiful. That was why he'd been late, that was why he'd spilled his food, that was why he'd made all the dumb jokes. I warmed to his honesty and willingness to be vulnerable, and I accepted a second date.

I was head-over-heels in love with him before the end of the month.

I pulled myself back to the here and now. *No*. I couldn't go there. Dan was gone. I'd moved on, found a type of peace. I wanted the next chapter in my life.

I wanted my next love.

Maybe Paige was right? Maybe Ryan could be that guy?

AFTER WE'D CLOSED the café for the day, Paige sat at her computer as I worked out what we needed for Cozy Cottage Catering's very first job coming up on Monday lunchtime. I'd just added a couple of items to the list when Paige made another one of her excited squeals.

"What's up?"

"We've got another email asking us to quote for another catering job!"

"Awesome!" I walked around the counter and peered over her shoulder at the screen. "It's a private party at someone's house? That's great."

"Yes, and it's only five days away. That's not a lot of notice."

"Their caterer must have let them down. Why don't you call the number they've given and ask them what they want? We've got enough time to pull something together for them. We've only got one other job on right now."

"And Cassie and Will's wedding."

"Which isn't for three months."

She laughed. "Okay. I'm on it."

I went back to work while Paige made the call. After a few moments, a knock at the back door interrupted me.

A seed of hope that it was Ryan grew as I walked over to the door and pulled it open. It wasn't Ryan. It was Sophie, dressed in a pair of jeans and a T-shirt, and she had someone with her.

My eyes moved from Sophie to the guy standing at her side. My jaw slackened, and my heart began to thud in my chest. Sure, he was tall and good looking, with dark hair and a big smile. He was probably a handful of years younger than me and had an air of confidence I could sense the moment I laid eyes on him.

But that wasn't what made me react the way I did. It was *who* he looked like that got me, right in the heart.

Dan.

From the curve of his smile to the deep blue of his eyes, he was

Dan's doppelgänger, through and through. Only here right now, standing in front of me. Alive.

Breathing.

"Hey, Bailey." The brightness of Sophie's voice was at odds with my internal turmoil.

"S-sophie." I tried to pull myself together. "You're not scheduled on until Tuesday."

"I know. I wanted you to meet my roommate, Jason. You know, the one I told you about?"

I nodded dumbly.

"Jason Christie, meet Bailey De Luca."

"Hey," the guy said, offering me his hand. "Great to meet you."

I took it and we shook. "It's ah, nice to meet you, too." I didn't look up into his eyes.

"I wanted to bring him down to meet you before Monday," Sophie said.

Monday. Catering job. Of course.

"Right."

Sophie shot me a questioning look. "You okay there? You look like you've seen a ghost."

It sure felt like I'd seen one.

"Yes, I'm totally fine. My mind is just on different things, that's all."

I glanced back at Jason. His face creased up into that smile again, and I swear I was back at Dan's apartment, talking and laughing with him, cuddled up on his sofa.

Only I was here, at the café, with a stranger who only looked like the man I once loved.

I had to pull myself out of this.

"I'm going to leave you to it. People to see, places to go." Sophie shot me a smile. "You two be good, now." She waggled her eyebrows at me.

I stifled a gasp. If Sophie knew the emotional rollercoaster I was on right now, I'm sure she wouldn't be so flippant.

"Sorry about my roommate," Jason said with a chuckle once

Sophie had waltzed down the alleyway toward the street. "She's got some crazy idea you're looking for a man, and I could be him."

Well, he was a straight shooter.

I crossed my arms over my chest and let out a laugh. It sounded forced, unnatural, even to my ears. "I'm looking for a *waiter*, that's what she means."

"Sure." He paused, still standing on the back step. "Should I maybe come in?"

"Oh, yes. Of course." I wrung my hands as I stood back. He brushed by me into the kitchen.

"So, this is where it all happens, huh? I love your food, although I can't afford to eat here much these days."

"Medical school, right?"

He nodded. "For my sins."

Paige walked back into the kitchen, phone in hand. "Oh, hi there."

I made the introductions, explaining who Jason was and why he was there. I concentrated on avoiding eye contact with him. But my belly twisted into an elaborate knot, my mind taking me places I couldn't go.

"Well, we're going to need you on Monday for lunch and next Saturday night for a party." Paige grinned.

"We got it?" I asked her.

"Sure did. Cozy Cottage Catering is a-go."

"Sounds good to me," Jason said. "I can do Saturday night as well as Monday. I could really do with the spare cash, so anything you've got, I'd be happy to take it on."

Even his voice sounded like Dan's. It all became too much for me.

"Paige? Why don't you take Dan-*Jason* through what we need him to do Monday? I've got to . . . do . . . something."

Like get out of here, stat!

"Sure. No problem." Her tone was uncertain, questioning.

I ignored the look she shot me as I collected my purse and jacket. "See you later!" Without glancing back, I pushed through the door, out into the warm afternoon sun. I darted up the alley and out onto the street, gulping deep breaths.

I hurried down the street, dodging groups of people out enjoying the sun, my need to get far away pressing on me. I kept walking, two blocks, three, four, until I reached my destination—a small park with a few benches scattered around by mature, leafy trees. I found a spare bench seat and dropped down.

I bit my lip and drummed my fingers on the wood.

An image of Dan's face clouded my mind. In an instant, we were back at my cottage after I'd come off a bicycle. Dan had been trying to transfer his love of mountain biking to me, and I'd given it a shot—with mixed results.

I could see myself sitting on my sofa, my leg stretched out in front of me. Dan had a bag of frozen peas in his hand, which he had wrapped in a tea towel and applied to my swollen ankle.

"It's only sprained. We need to keep it elevated like this and apply ice for ten minutes. Do you think you can do that?"

I nodded.

"Here." He took my hand and placed it on top of the bag of peas, stood up, and walked in the direction of the front door.

I shot him a confused look. "Aren't you going to stay?"

"I'll be back in ten minutes."

The door closed behind him, and I was left on my sofa, wondering what my boyfriend of five months thought was more important right now than being here with me. Before the ten minutes were up, he let himself back into the house, balancing some items in his hands.

"I thought you could do with a few things. Here's a cup of coffee from that café we both like down the road." He placed a takeout cup on the coffee table. "A bar of your favorite chocolate." He held up a magazine. "And a magazine about dresses or movie stars or diets you girls seem to like so much."

I beamed, my heart full. "I'm probably less interested in the diet part. You're the best boyfriend, you know that?"

"Oh, I almost forgot the most important thing."

"What?"

He dropped down beside me, lifted my chin with his fingers, and kissed me. "That."

"Of all these things—" I gestured at the items he'd put on my coffee table, "I think I like that part the best."

"Yeah," he replied, his eyes soft. "Me too."

A child's sharp cry pulled me back to the present.

Jason. His name was Jason. He was just a guy who was doing some casual work for us.

My brain knew it wasn't Dan. I knew it was only a guy who happened to look like Dan—*just like him*—who reminded me of what we'd had together.

Of what I'd lost.

This was nothing more than a jolt from the past. I could deal with this.

Totally.

Didn't I get a similar jolt whenever I saw Josh, his brother? Or when I saw his mum, Meredith? Although that happened less and less now that Paige had replaced her as my partner in the Cozy Cottage.

No. It meant nothing. It was just an echo, Dan was dead and gone. I'd moved on with my life.

I'd had to.

And having some guy who looked like him working for us was not going to change that.

Chapter 13

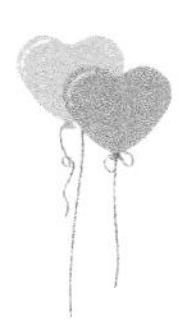

THE NEXT MORNING, MY phone beeped on the nightstand. I was sitting in bed, a cup of Earl Grey tea in hand, enjoying my one morning off in the week. I picked it up and read the screen. I smiled when I saw it was from Ryan.

Busy?

This was the first I'd heard from him since that sizzling make-out session on Friday night, and warmth spread across my chest.

Yes, doing very important things right now.

I took a sip of my tea and waited for his reply, dots appearing on the screen. I didn't have to wait long.

Can I interrupt those things?

Depends what you had in mind.

I want a rematch.

I let out a light laugh. Friday night had started out so badly with Fake Jamie and ended quite the opposite with Ryan.

Before I had the chance to reply, my phone beeped again.

Either that or a real game.

Baseball?

Tennis.

Although I hadn't picked up a racket in some time, I'd played tennis all through high school, and I was pretty good, representing my school and club. I fired off a text, complete with tennis player emojis, a boy player and a girl player.

You're on.

Pick you up in an hour.

Fifty-eight minutes later, I'd managed to dig out my old tennis skirt and top, discovered to my glee they still fitted, and found my racket right at the back of my hallway closet. I knew I'd be rusty, but I wanted to at least manage to hold my own, so I did a few practice shots with a flat ball against the wall at the back of my cottage.

Let's just say it didn't instill a lot of confidence in my abilities.

The doorbell rang, making me jump. It's funny how you can be waiting for someone to arrive, and when they do, you still get a surprise.

I opened the door to see Ryan standing in a pair of sports shorts and a white T that accentuated his muscular physique and wide shoulders, a black cap with a silver fern on his head. His grin was wide, making him even more handsome—not that I'd thought that was even possible.

"Ready to be humiliated on the court, De Luca?" His eyes twinkled.

"The question is, are *you* ready? I mean, if your delicate male ego can take another beating, that is."

He laughed, and I wished he'd kiss me. "Fighting talk, De Luca. Fighting talk."

I picked up my tennis bag and slung it over my shoulder, collected my keys from the hallway table, and stepped outside into the morning sun.

Once in Ryan's SUV, we chatted about tennis, and I began to get seriously concerned Ryan was a lot better than just a "handy" player, as he'd referred to himself on Friday night. A short drive later, we arrived at some tennis courts I had passed many times but never actually played on.

All but one of the courts was in use, so we walked to the back court where we both dropped our bags on the ground and pulled out our rackets. Ryan opened a fresh can of balls, and we went to opposite ends of the court, ready to play.

"I'll go easy on you to begin with," Ryan said, bouncing one of the balls on the ground. "But then I may have to release the fury."

"The fury?" I questioned with a laugh.

"Oh, I'm famous for it."

"So, I should be afraid?"

"You just wait and see."

I walked around the net to my end of the court. Ryan got himself into position to serve and bounced the ball a few times with his hand.

"Do you think you're Novak Djokovic or someone?" I teased, referring to how the famous tennis player always bounced the ball a bunch of times before serving.

Instead of responding, he fired a serve down the court—and straight past me.

Uh-oh. I'm in trouble.

"Shall we warm up first? That was probably just me showing off."

"Probably?"

"Okay, definitely. Let's just hit the ball around for a while, then we can see if we want to play a game, 'kay?"

"Sure."

He pulled another ball out of his pocket and served it to me. This time, thankfully, the shot was a lot less bullet-like in its delivery. I hit it back, enjoying the *thwack* of my racket making contact with the ball, and we started a rally.

From that initial serve, I knew he was going easy on me, but I was okay with that. I valued my dignity, and if that serve was anything to go by, it would be in total tatters within minutes if he pulled out his A-game.

After warming up and growing my confidence, I suggested we play an actual game.

"You serve," he called out as he batted the balls down to my end of the court.

I collected them up, stuffing a couple of them up the built-in shorts of my tennis skirt, ready to be pulled out when needed. I got myself into position, lined the court up, threw the ball into the air and hit it, watching as it landed within the service lines on Ryan's side. He hit it back, right by the service line, and I had to run to get it, sneaking it over the net for a winner.

"Lucky shot."

We continued to play, me taking the game in deuce. Then it was Ryan's turn to serve. We switched court ends, as was the custom in tennis, and he waggled his eyebrows at me as he walked passed. "You ready for this?"

"Go easy on me," I pleaded with a flirty smile.

And he did. His serve was strong and confident, and we had some great rallies. He won the game comfortably, but I didn't mind. It was clear he was the much better player. I could live with that.

We played a few more games until I called for a drinks break, my body screaming at me that it had had enough. With the amount of time the café takes up, I didn't get much of a chance to exercise these days. Well, it was either that or the large amount of cake I got to eat most days.

With our backs leaning up against the wire fence, we drank from our water bottles. My forehead was sweaty, and I wiped it with my wristband, thankful I'd remembered to sweep my hair up in a high ponytail.

"You know, you're not a bad player," Ryan said.

"Not quite as good as you."

"Well, you can't be good at everything, can you? You are the reigning Wii Baseball champ."

"That's true. Where's my trophy, by the way? And my sash? I'm definitely going to need one of those."

He laughed. "I'll see what I can do." He turned to face me, leaning his shoulder against the fence. He reached out and took me by the hand. "There's this thing I've got to go to on Friday night. It's a ball, quite a fancy thing, I guess."

I hoped I knew where he was going with this. "Yes?"

"I was wondering. Will you come with me? I mean, I know you have your concert thing, so you might not be able to."

I pushed myself off the fence and squeezed his hand. "Ryan, I'd love to." An image of a fairytale ball, Ryan as the dashing prince, and me in a gorgeous, shimmering gown, flashed before my eyes.

He smiled at me. "Great. It's formal, so you'll need a dress."

"I've got dresses." In fact, virtually my entire wardrobe was dresses, thanks to my obsession with vintage 'fifties clothing. "And don't worry about the Jam. The Cozy Cottage will survive without me for one night."

"Good. I guess it's a date, then," he said with a grin.

I could almost hear Paige's voice in my head. *A Last First Date?*

I smiled back. "I guess it is."

Chapter 14

THE FIRST THING I did when I got home from my tennis match with Ryan was pull all my evening dresses out from my closet, lay them on my bed, and run a critical eye over them. I mean, it's not like a girl got invited to a *ball* every day of the week, was it?

By the time I'd looked them all over, I'd determined they were either not dressy enough, not the right length, too conservative, or simply not "wow" enough for a Last First Date.

Because that's what I had allowed myself to think this was.

And I was terrified and totally excited about it in equal measure.

No one had made me feel the way Ryan did for a long, long time. Not since Dan had butterflies twirled in my belly, such enjoyment from simply being with someone. I couldn't stop myself from smiling whenever I thought of him, warmth spreading through me.

And the kissing? Well, I hadn't had anything to match that, either.

Not that I'd kissed anyone else since Dan had passed away, so there was probably not a lot to compare it with. But still.

Since this was our first real date together, I wanted to look the best I could. So far, none of the dresses I had laid out on my bed came anywhere close.

Nevertheless, I tried a few of them on, hoping one of them might work. You know how sometimes a dress looks quite average on a hanger and amazing on? Didn't happen. Not one fit the bill. They were all perfectly nice, and I'd been happy to wear each and every one of them in the past, but because this was my Last First Date, the dress I wore on this date needed to be extra special.

After all, one day I hoped to tell our grandchildren all about the magical first date I went on with their grandpop. Who knew? Maybe one day, one of our granddaughters would wear the dress I chose for the ball on *her* Last First Date?

But then again, maybe I was getting a little ahead of myself.

I stood with my arms crossed, tapping my chin with my index finger, trying to work out what to do. Should I buy a new dress? Should I pull out my sewing skills—which were poor at best—and make something?

And then it struck me.

I rushed out of my bedroom and down the hall. I pulled the door open to my small garage. There was a stack of boxes on one side, placed on top of an old leather travel trunk. I set to it unstacking the boxes. I wanted what I knew was in the trunk, something Nona had left me.

You see, Nona had been quite the debutante in her day, back in Italy. She'd left me several dresses she'd worn going to fabulous balls and parties back in the 'fifties, which she'd had wrapped in acid-free paper and stored in the old travel trunk.

Something told me I would be able to find what I was looking for in there.

Ten minutes, the boxes moved, and much ferreting through the old trunk later, I'd found the perfect dress. I knew it the moment I clapped eyes on it.

I unwrapped it carefully from its tissue paper and held it up against myself. It was the usual 'fifties cut with a nipped in waist and full skirt, complete with petticoats, falling mid-calf on me. The boned top was strapless with a heart-shaped neckline.

Right there in my garage, I ripped my tennis gear off and

slipped the dress over my head. It had a back zipper, which was tricky to do up on my own of course, but it fit perfectly.

I rushed through the house to look at my reflection in the long lean-to mirror in my bedroom. I took in the cut of the dress, the way it showed off my curves in a thoroughly classy way, the nipped in waist accentuating my hour-glass figure. It was made of exquisite royal blue silk, and it rustled as I moved.

As I looked at my reflection, I knew this was the right dress for the ball.

I let out a contented sigh. The dress was perfect, the man was perfect. I knew the evening would be perfect, too.

I felt like a princess.

Yes, this is the dress.

THE FOLLOWING DAY, Paige and I left Sophie in charge of the café to go on our very first Cozy Cottage Catering job. It was only a light lunch and finger food for twelve members of a board, who were meeting at a location downtown. But as it was our first, we were treating it as though we were catering to royalty.

We were due to meet Jason at the venue, a high-rise building in the center of town, and I'll admit I was more nervous about seeing him than I was about the job. He'd been playing on my mind since we met a couple of days ago.

"Can you to tell me what happened on Saturday afternoon? You know, after you left so suddenly when Jason came to the café?" Paige asked as I drove us through the busy city streets to the hotel.

I came to a stop at a set of traffic lights. "I guess."

"Come on, Bailey. You can tell me. I've been trying to work it out and I came up with one possibility."

I glanced at my friend in the passenger seat. Her face was creased in concern for me, and I had a sudden desire to come clean with her.

"I know this is going to sound really stupid, and I'm kind of embarrassed. But the thing is, Jason reminded me of someone." I tightened my grip on the steering wheel.

"Dan." Paige's voice was soft.

I snapped my head in her direction. "How did you know?"

"After you left, Josh came by to pick me up and he said the same thing. He said it gave him a shock to see someone who looked so much like his brother."

"Oh."

"Look, why don't you drop me and the food at the venue? Jason and I can manage just fine without you."

I shot her a smile. Paige was such a sweet friend and her kindness had me blinking back the tears—not exactly a good thing when driving through the thick traffic in New Zealand's busiest city.

As tempting as her offer was, I didn't want to be a coward. I'd be seeing Jason again on Saturday. I needed to "woman-up" here.

"That's really thoughtful of you, Paige, but no. I'll do it. It was just the initial shock, that's all. I'll be fine."

Truth be told, I wasn't particularly fine. The moment I laid eyes on Jason, dressed in a pair of black pants and white shirt, looking every inch the high-end waiter we'd instructed him to be, my tummy tied in knots, and I had to resist the strong urge to run again.

Paige took the lead with him, telling him what we needed him to do, giving me the chance to hide out, busying myself with the food prep. Which is what I did, spending the entirety of the job managing to avoid looking at him.

I probably came across as some sort of weirdo, but I didn't care. This was survival, people! Well, at least until I got used to having the spitting image of my former fiancé around.

In the lobby afterwards, the executive assistant to the board, a nice woman in her twenties called Joanne, sang our praises. "That was delicious! Thank you so much. Judging by the fact all the food went, I think the silver foxes loved it, too."

Paige and I laughed. "The silver foxes?" Paige asked.

It was true the board members had all been older men, so the name was fitting.

"Yeah." Joanne laughed. "They may not all be foxes, but they like it when I call them that."

"Well, we're very pleased to hear they all liked the lunch. I hope you think of us next time you need a caterer."

"Oh, absolutely. In fact," she pulled her phone out of her pocket and began to tap her screen, "can you do the twenty-fifth? The silver foxes are having a get together at the chairman's place. We'd need a dinner for about thirty?"

I beamed, shooting Paige a look. "That sounds great. I'll book it into the calendar and be back in touch about the details."

"Fabulous, thanks." Joanne's heels clicked on the polished floor as she walked across the lobby.

The elevator pinged, and Jason stepped out, holding a stack of trays. He smiled at Joanne and said something to her that made her laugh. As he walked over toward Paige and me, she turned and mouthed what appeared to be "so cute," before she disappeared into the elevator.

"Where do you want these, ladies?" Jason asked.

Paige answered while I concentrated on studying the floor.

Man, I needed to get over this! He wasn't Dan. He was Jason Christie, medical student and now part-time waiter at Cozy Cottage Catering.

"Bailey?" Paige said.

I snapped my head up. "What?"

"I was just saying Jason can put the trays in the trunk, once you've brought the car around."

"Oh, yes. Of course." I chanced a look at Jason. He was watching me with a questioning look on his face.

What must he think of me?

"I'll go get the car now." I turned on my heel and pushed my way through the revolving doors out onto the street.

Maybe the Universe was using Jason to test me, to make sure I'd moved on from Dan?

I could conquer this, I knew I could.

Chapter 15

FRIDAY NIGHT SEEMED LIKE it took months to come around. I'd spent the week as I always did, working at the café. Only this week, Paige and I were riding high on our catering company success, our optimism filling the air around us.

Finally, after Paige insisted for the third time she and Sophie had everything under control for the Cozy Cottage Jam, I collected my purse, ready to leave.

"Have an amazing time," Paige said, giving me a hug.

Sophie slouched against the wall. "I wish it was me."

I couldn't blame her for having a crush on Ryan. He was handsome and charming, the kind of guy a lot of women wanted to be with.

But he was mine. Or, if he wasn't yet, he would be very soon.

"Oh, Soph. You'll find your guy," Paige said, rubbing her arm.

"Yeah? When? I've kissed so many frogs I could ribbit."

"Ribbit?"

"You know, like a frog," Sophie replied glumly. "Ribbit, ribbit."

"You'll meet someone, honey. All in good time," Paige replied.

Sophie let out a laugh. "You sound like my mother."

I laughed, too, shaking my head. "Soph's right, you kinda do."

"Well, maybe I just have a feeling about these things? I did about Ryan and Bailey, you know."

Paige had always been a little quirky, believing in fate and the mystery of the world, the universe, and everything. She believed things happened for a reason—not a view I shared. What was the reason for Dan dying at the age of twenty-nine?

"Maybe you do have a third eye, or whatever they call it, Paige. But right now, I've got to go get myself into a rather fabulous dress for my date."

I couldn't stop a surge of excitement at the prospect. I'd had Nona's dress cleaned, and it was good to go, hanging on the door of my closest, the necklace and shoes I'd chosen sitting beside it.

"You'll look beautiful. You always do," Sophie said.

"Just be sure to have an amazing time," Paige added.

"Thanks, ladies. See you tomorrow."

"I'll open up in the morning. You get here when you can."

I pulled the back door open and flashed them a grin. "Thanks."

At home, I showered and did my makeup, sweeping black liquid eyeliner over my eyelids in keeping with the 'fifties vibe of the dress. I applied my red lipstick and smacked my lips together, studying my reflection. I'd left my long hair loose, taming the curls into waves that framed my face. Nona had always said I looked like screen siren Sofia Loren in her heyday when I got myself dressed up. As I looked at my reflection, I thought she may have been onto something, although I knew I would pale in comparison against the real thing.

I stepped into the dress and pulled it up. I'd loosely attached a piece of ribbon to the zipper so I could zip it up the whole way on my own, and it worked perfectly. I adjusted the dress, did the clasp on my necklace, and slipped my feet into a pair of patent leather black heels. I regarded myself in the mirror, swooshing the dress from side to side.

I was a fairy princess on my way to the ball with my very own Prince Charming.

As if on cue, the doorbell rang and those belly butterflies that always batted their wings when Ryan was around turned up. I collected my silver clutch from the bed and walked down the hall to the front door.

I pulled the door open to see him standing there, dressed in a tux with a crisp white shirt, a grin spread across his handsome face. My breath caught in my throat at the sight of him. If I was a princess tonight, he was most certainly my dashing prince. All we needed was a horse and carriage and perhaps a coachman or two and we'd be living our own personal fairytale.

"Wow, Bailey, you look . . . so beautiful."

My body tingled as Ryan's eyes swept over me. I beamed at him. "Thanks. You look amazing in your tux."

"Why, thank you." He waggled his eyebrows at me. "Are you ready to go, *Mademoiselle*?"

"I sure am."

"Well, then in that case, your chariot awaits." He extended his arm and I took it.

I let out a light laugh, lapping up the fairytale atmosphere. I closed and locked the door behind me and we walked down the path, arm in arm.

I stopped in my tracks when I saw the car parked on the side of the street. My eyes widened. "*That's* the chariot? I assumed it'd be your SUV." I took in the car in the early evening light. It was a fancy, old fashioned looking car, probably a Morgan or a Jag or something—I was no petrol head. Whatever it was, it was classy and oh-so romantic.

"Nothing but the best for you tonight."

I looked up into Ryan's eyes, the butterflies doing overtime. "It's perfect, Ryan. Thank you."

The driver's door opened and a man in a suit and driver's cap stepped out onto the curb.

"Will?" I blinked at him, barely believing my eyes.

"You can call me Jeeves for the night, if you like," he said with a little bow, flashing us his cheeky grin.

I let out an excited laugh. "All right, *Jeeves*."

I looked back at Ryan. "You're wonderful, you know that?"

He smiled, the skin around his eyes crinkling. "You're worth it."

Be still my beating heart!

Ryan was proving to be every inch the man of my dreams tonight. And the evening had only just begun.

Will opened the car door for me and I thanked him and slipped inside, scooting across the seat for Ryan to sit next to me. The interior of the car was just as I'd imagined—tan leather, walnut trim, and old-fashioned window handles. Ryan took my hand in his, and Will drove us downtown to the five-star hotel where the ball was being held.

A short journey later, we arrived at the front door of the hotel. Will "Jeeves" Jordan parked the car and walked around to open my door.

"Thank you, Jeeves," I said, smiling as I stepped out onto a red carpet leading up the steps into the hotel lobby.

"Certainly, madam."

He was really getting into this whole chauffeur thing.

Ryan offered me his arm once more, and we walked up the steps and into the hotel. I looked back at Will and waved. He winked at me then got into the car and slowly drove away.

"How did you talk Will into doing that for us?"

"I bumped into him at the suit hire place. He was getting his tux for his wedding, and he asked me what I needed one for. When I told him, he offered to help out. Apparently, Paige and Cassie had been talking about us."

"Hmm, I bet. I never had Will Jordan pegged as a romantic, though." I shook my head. Cassie was a lucky girl.

I glanced at Ryan. Not as lucky as me, though. "And the car?"

"That belongs to my parents' wealthy neighbor. I have to get it back to him tomorrow in one piece on pain of death."

"Let's hope Will doesn't do anything silly, then."

We walked down a wide corridor to double wooden doors, the words "Renoir Suite" above the entrance in gold lettering. Music was floating out, and I could hear the muffled sounds of chatter and laughter from behind the doors.

"We're here." Ryan pulled one of the doors open for me and I stepped inside.

It was a large room, with a band playing 'forties swing music on a stage at the far end, massive crystal chandeliers hanging from the ceiling. There was a dance floor, empty right now, and people were dressed in ball gowns and tuxes, chatting and laughing together.

"This is . . . perfect," I murmured, more to myself than anyone else.

Ryan slid his arm around my waist and leant in toward me. "*You're* perfect."

I looked up at him and blushed. "No, not at all. But this?" I gazed around the room.

"It's going to be a fun night. Come on, let's get a drink. Champagne?"

I nodded. "Oh, yes."

What other drink could we possibly have on a night like this?

We got our drinks and Ryan spotted some people he knew over by one of the tables. He introduced me, and I ended up chatting to one of the women about Italian food and how important it was to use fresh tomatoes in sauces, not canned. Something Nona taught me, naturally.

After a while, dinner was announced, and we found our table, sitting with some of Ryan's colleagues. I didn't know anyone, but people were friendly. I watched Ryan, relaxed and easy-going, chatting and laughing with everyone.

Dinner was a delicious hot smoked salmon salad followed by tuna steaks, and then an emcee announced the awards portion of the evening.

"Are you nominated for anything?" I asked Ryan.

"Not this year, although my firm won 'Best New Design' last year for a project I co-led."

"That's amazing. Maybe next year, huh?"

He squeezed my hand under the table. "Maybe next year. Actually, we found out today we've just won some business. I'm going to be part of a team designing a new building for national art treasures."

"That's wonderful!"

"We're breaking ground in about a month, on the twenty-sixth, actually. It's a bit of thing, you know? The owners, the media. I might even be in the news."

"Really?" I tapped my foot against my chair leg.

"If you'd like to come, we could go for a late lunch afterwards?"

"Sounds great." I feigned a smile.

The twenty-sixth of next month had particular meaning for me, too. It was the anniversary of Dan's death. Three years. I swallowed, trying to concentrate on the speeches. I couldn't think about that now, not on such an enchanted evening as this.

The awards ceremony went on for quite some time, and I swear my hands grew numb through clapping. The final award had been announced, and the band started up once more, people pouring onto the dancefloor.

"Are you going to ask me to dance?" I said to Ryan.

"Are you going to say yes if I do?"

"Yes."

"Then, yes. Bailey, will you dance with me?" He stood up and offered his hand.

I took it with a smile, and we walked to the dancefloor where Ryan held me in his arms. It felt nice. *More* than nice. He twirled and dipped me, making my head spin—although that could have been from the champagne, too. I was definitely a cheap drunk, the two glasses I'd had over dinner more than enough to make me a little tipsy.

The music changed to a slower song, and Ryan pulled me in closer, his big hands pressed into the small of my back. I breathed in his delicious Ryan scent, wrapping my arms around his neck.

"Are you having fun?"

"I'm having the best time." I looked up into his eyes.

"Good." He bent his head down and kissed me lightly on the lips. "Me too," he murmured in my ear, his breath warm on my neck.

I let out a sigh. I wanted this, I *needed* this.

We swayed to the music, our bodies as one. I couldn't imagine the night being any more perfect than it was.

The tempo of the next song changed back again, and I

suggested we sit this one out. My shoes may be gorgeous, but they were killing my toes.

We sat down at our table, all the chairs around us empty but for a couple all cozied up on the other side. Ryan raised his chin at them in greeting and we took our seats.

He leaned in to me, his elbows on his knees. "Bailey, I need to tell you something."

"Sure. What is it?"

"You know that thing I said about wanting to kiss you for so long and not doing anything about it?"

A smile curved my lips. "Oh, that."

"I thought I should tell you why."

I sat up in my seat. "Okay."

"I guess it was because . . . well, I was still working through some stuff, you know, after my break-up."

I nodded, recalling the shell of a man he was when I'd first met him.

"I know this is going to feel a bit sappy, but I guess I didn't want you to be a rebound girl."

My heart rate kicked up. "You didn't?"

He shook his head. "No." He placed his fingers under my chin and leaned in and kissed me once more. It was soft and sweet, full of the promise of what could be between us.

We leant our foreheads against one another.

"I want you to be more than just that."

I pulled away to look him in the eyes. "Because this feels big."

He nodded, pressing his lips together. "It does to me."

I put my hands on his chest and looked into his eyes. "You know what? You're worth waiting for, Ryan Jones."

And I knew he was.

Chapter 16

IT WAS OFFICIAL: I was on Cloud Nine. And oh, my, did I like being there. I floated from home to work, to seeing Ryan, and back again. And it kept on getting better and better. We'd been out to dinner, played some more tennis (I won this time, but I'm certain he let me), and just simply been hanging out, enjoying one another's company. He was sweet and thoughtful, and I found myself wanting to spend all my free time with him—which wasn't a lot of time when you ran a busy city café and catering company.

Not that the catering business had quite taken off as much as Paige and I would have liked. Although we'd been contacted on our website about many jobs since our first one for Joanne's "silver foxes," we were finding that we weren't winning new business very often.

I sat in the café kitchen at my laptop and checked our emails. My face dropped when I saw a message from Joanne. "Oh, no."

Paige looked up at me from the carrot cake she was icing with cream cheese frosting. "What is it?"

"Joanne no longer wants us to cater her 'silver foxes' party this weekend."

"What? Why?"

I scanned the rest of the email. "She said they had another catering firm approach them and decided to give them the party. She didn't say why, exactly. She was very nice about it, but still."

"Well, that's annoying. But you know what? It's just a matter of time, Bailey. Word's going to get out how good we are, how great our food is. Have faith, okay?"

I smiled at her, wishing I had her optimism. Of the fourteen requests for quotes that had come in over the past few weeks, we'd only won two of them, and now we'd lost Joanne's party. Those were not good odds in anyone's books.

"Do you think it's something to do with our marketing?"

"No, the marketing's great. And we know they love our food. Just be patient, okay?" Paige picked a knife up and began to slice the cake.

"I guess." I collected the keys to the front door and wandered out into the café, flicking the lights on. There were already a couple of people waiting outside, and as I unlocked and opened the door, I greeted them with a "good morning" and set about serving them at the counter. At this time of day, the most anyone wanted was a takeout cup of coffee and maybe a breakfast muffin, so they were on their way before too long, happily caffeinated.

"Could you open the cabinet, please?" Paige was holding a freshly iced flourless chocolate and raspberry drizzle cake in her hands.

"Sure." I pulled the door open and rearranged the cakes already inside so she could fit the new addition.

She slid it inside before I closed up again.

"I've been thinking. How about I call some of the jobs we didn't get and ask them why they chose someone else?"

Paige nodded. "That's good market research. Make sure you mention that when you call them, otherwise they might think you're just being nosey. Want to do it now?"

"Sure thing. Call out if you need me. Sophie should be here any minute."

I sat at the kitchen counter and opened my laptop, finding the list of email enquiries we'd received on the website. I clicked on the contact details for someone at Nettco Electricity, a woman by the name of Beth Matson. I pulled out my phone and dialed her number. She answered almost immediately.

"Jennifer Carlisle's office, Beth speaking."

"Hi, Beth. This is Bailey De Luca from Cozy Cottage Catering. You enquired about us catering a function?"

"Yes, that's right," she replied brightly. "But I'm sorry, we gave the business to another caterer."

"That's why I'm calling. You see we're doing some market research," I thought Paige would be proud, "and it would be really helpful if you could tell us why you chose not to use us."

"Why?" Her tone changed. Gone was the bright and friendly voice from seconds earlier.

I had to do some quick thinking. Working in the hospitality industry had taught me a thing or two about customer service. "So we can make sure we get it right the next time." I held my breath, waiting for her to respond, half expecting her to hang up on me. I don't know why I thought that, exactly—people can be irrational, can't they? "We'd really appreciate your help," I added as a last-ditch attempt.

"Oh, all right, but only because us girls need to stick together."

I sat and listened to Beth as she told me all about how her boyfriend had done the dirty on her and how all men were idiots, particularly her ex. Eventually, after lots of "I hear you" and "that's terrible" from me, she got to the crux of the conversation.

"We gave it to another place called Devour Catering. They said they could do the same type of menu as you, discounted by twenty percent. I remember he called it his 'Cozy Mansion' offer. A weak play on words if you ask me, but we couldn't pass up that twenty percent discount."

Cozy Mansion? I tapped my foot against the chair leg.

"Did you share our menu with them?" I tried not to sound as aghast as I felt.

"Heck, no! As I said, we girls have to stick together."

I had stopped myself from pointing out that Beth hadn't exactly stuck with us.

"He was pretty smooth, too. Good looking in a kinda sleazy way, if that makes sense?"

"Do you remember his name?"

"Hold on, I'll get his card."

As Beth rustled through papers, I tapped my chin. Calling their offer the "Cozy Mansion," discounting our prices by twenty percent? I may have been jumping to conclusions, but it felt like we were being targeted. Only, I had no clue how.

"Here it is. Eddie Smith."

I'd never heard of Eddie Smith.

"Thank you so much, Beth. You've been really helpful."

I hung up and immediately called one of the other contact numbers. Six phone calls later, and I started to get a picture of what was going on. And I wasn't happy about it.

I snapped the laptop shut and walked out into the café. Sophie was working the coffee machine and Paige was serving a line of customers. I dove in to help, shelving my conspiracy theory for later when I could speak with Paige alone.

That time came later in the day, once the lunch rush was over and the café had begun to wind down for the day.

"And was it the same catering company every time?" Paige had an incredulous look on her face.

"It sure was. It's called Devour."

"Oh, my gosh, I've heard of them!"

"It's run by a guy called Eddie Smith."

"Eddie Smith?" Paige shook her head. "Not a name I know."

"Me neither. It's not surprising though, is it? We've only been caterers for the last few weeks."

"But why would he target us with this 'Cozy Mansion' thing? I don't get it. It's not like we're the big fish here. We're a new start-up business, with hardly any experience."

"Exactly. How could he know who has contacted us for quotes?"

"Hold on a second." Paige walked over to the counter and opened my laptop. She tapped on the keyboard, her brows knitted together in concentration. After ten seconds focusing at the screen, she leaned back on her heels and looked at me, her face aghast. "Oh, no."

"What is it?" I peered over her shoulder at the screen. It was the catering contact page on our website Paige had shown me when she set it up. My eyes trailed down the screen. I let out a gasp. "Oh, no," I echoed.

Every one of the people who had contacted us for catering quotes were listed on the page, with their requests, email addresses, and requirements. We'd inadvertently advertised all our potential clients to the world on one page!

Paige's eyes bulged, worry written across her face. "Bailey, I'm so, *so* sorry. This part is meant to be private. I must have messed it up somehow." She clicked onto another screen and started tapping away on the keyboard once more.

"How did it happen?"

"I don't know, but I'll fix it . . . somehow."

I let out a heavy sigh. "Well, at least we know how this Eddie Smith guy got the information. I guess that's something, at least."

Paige stopped tapping and turned to me, her eyes wide. "That's true, but what we don't know is *why*."

She had a point, and I was determined to find the answer.

LATER THAT AFTERNOON, I sat in front of my laptop researching Devour Catering and Eddie Smith. Although I found Devour's site, with all its slick presentation and elegant photography, I couldn't find a single piece of information on Eddie Smith.

He was an enigma, that was for sure. An enigma who had targeted our new business for no apparent reason.

I looked up from my screen to see Paige coming into the kitchen, followed by Marissa.

"Hi, Marissa." I wondered what she was doing here at this time of day—and why she was in the kitchen. Usually she and Cassie came in for coffee and cake mid-morning, sitting at their favorite table by the window.

"Hey." Her smile seemed forced, unnatural.

"I'll leave you two to it. I've got customers to serve." Paige threw me a look before she left the room.

I knitted my brows together. "What's up?" There was no point in any preamble.

"Look, there's no easy way to put this so I'll just come out and say it."

I closed my laptop. "Okay."

"I'm not sure you should date Ryan."

I bit my lip. I should have seen this coming. Marissa had warned me off Ryan when I first met him and again not that long ago. She'd told me he was a broken man, totally messed up about women—all thanks to his ex. To be frank, I was kind of surprised she hadn't mentioned him to me again in the weeks we'd been dating.

The problem was, I was beginning to develop feelings for him, feelings I hadn't had for anyone in a very long time.

"Look, Marissa, I know what you're going to say. You think he's all messed up over his ex. We've talked about it, and I really think he's moved on. He's good. *We're* good." I smiled at the thought of Ryan—and the way he made me feel.

She drew her lips into a thin line, studying me. "I'm not so sure about that."

"I know he's your brother and you want to look out for him. I totally get that. But so far it's all been great."

Marissa opened her mouth to respond when there was a loud rap on the back door.

I put my finger in the air. "Hold that thought, okay?"

She nodded, and I walked over to the door and opened it.

"Hello, Bailey," said an elegant older woman in a pants suit and string of pearls.

My eyes widened, my heart thudding.

It was Meredith Bentley.

Dan's mother.

Chapter 17

"MEREDITH. IT'S SO NICE to see you." I gave her a brief hug. It was forced and unnatural, her body rigid.

A smile formed on her face. "Bailey. You look wonderful."

"Thanks. You do, too."

On the outside, I was smiling and composed.

Inside was a completely different story.

"Do you have a moment?" Meredith asked.

"Sure do." I turned back to Marissa. "Can we . . . pick this up later?"

Whatever "this" was.

"Of course." Marissa nodded. "I'll call you later."

I couldn't think about Marissa's warning not to date her brother right now. Seeing Meredith was like a foghorn going off in my brain, reminding me of my past—reminding me of Dan.

I shot Marissa a quick smile as she left the kitchen for the café. I returned my attention to Meredith, still standing at the door. She was never a large woman, keeping herself very "trim" as my mum would say. She was always nicely turned out, wearing beautifully tailored jackets, a string of Mikimoto pearls always around her neck.

Today was no exception, although there was something about

her, something I couldn't put my finger on. A type of tension in her features.

"Can we go somewhere to talk? I know you usually close up about this time. I thought you might be able to spare me a few minutes?"

"Oh, of course. I'll, ah, I'll just go and do a couple of things to close up. How about I meet you in fifteen minutes?"

She gave me a tight smile. "Wonderful. Where?"

I racked my brain for somewhere to go. Most of the cafés in the area closed at the same time as us. "There's a burger place open at this time of day over on Wallingworth Street."

I was certain Meredith hadn't set a refined foot in a burger joint for at least twenty years—if ever—but it was all I could think of on the spot. Her sudden appearance at the café had totally thrown me.

Seven minutes later, Paige had bustled me out of the café, insisting she could close the café up by herself, telling me I needed to do what I needed to do.

"Do you have any idea why she's here?" I slipped the strap of my purse over my shoulder. "I mean, when she was running the place with me we'd catch up every week, but I haven't seen her at all since you became my partner."

If anyone had the inside scoop behind Meredith's sudden appearance at the café, it would be Paige. She was dating Meredith's youngest son, after all.

She drew her eyebrows together. "I should have told you."

"Told me what?"

"Josh and I had dinner with her last night and she asked after you."

"And?"

"And I mentioned you had gone to the ball."

I chewed the inside of my lip. "She knows I'm dating someone?"

Paige nodded. "I'm really sorry if I put my foot in it, Bailey. I wanted her to know you're doing great, that's all."

First with the website mess up and now with this? Paige was outdoing herself today.

"I'm really sorry if I said something I shouldn't have."

"No, no. It'll be fine." I sounded at least twice as confident as I felt.

As I dashed passed the empty florist shop and down the street, my mind went into overdrive. Meredith and I used to be close. I'd gotten to know her when I began dating Dan, back when we were in our early twenties, back before everything went so horribly wrong. She shared my love of food, although unlike me, she ate like a bird, something I'd never been able to manage.

Still, she appreciated fine food, and was incredibly supportive of Dan and me when we decided to go into business together, opening the Cozy Cottage Café.

When Dan passed away, Meredith stepped in, buying Dan out. If she hadn't done so I would have lost the place. I was eternally in her debt. She'd told me at the time she didn't want me to lose my business as well as my fiancé. She never got involved in the day-to-day management, but the simple fact of her doing what she did was life saving for me.

I owed her a lot.

I pushed the heavy wooden door of the burger joint on Wallingworth Street open, my eyes adjusting to the darkness of the room.

A host wearing a pair of white pants and black T-shirt, a pair of bright red braces the only color in the outfit, materialized at my side. "Welcome to Gourmet Burgers. Can I get you a table?"

"Oh, I'm meeting someone. I think she's already here." I scanned the room, looking for Meredith.

"An older woman, looks like she belongs at a museum fundraiser?"

I smiled. She'd got her pegged. "That's the one."

"Right this way."

I followed her over to a table by a window overlooking a small courtyard.

Meredith looked up at me, still with that pinched expression on her face. "Bailey."

"I'll be right back to take your order."

I thanked the server and pulled out a chair, taking the seat opposite Meredith. "Hi again."

"Thank you for meeting me."

"Of course."

She looked so small and frail, I had the urge to collect her up in a hug—and then feed her a large meal.

"How have you been?"

"Oh, fine. Just fine. George and I've been away in Europe recently. We had a wonderful time, traveling around Italy. The lakes, Tuscany, Rome. You would have loved it. It was a shame you never made it there."

Dan and I had planned to go to Italy for our honeymoon. Despite my Italian heritage, I'd never been to Italy before.

I swallowed down the lump forming in my throat. "Yeah, I would have."

"I bought this while I was in Sicily." She produced a small, silk purse and handed it to me.

"Thank you." I opened the dome on the purse and pulled out a dark gray beaded necklace. "Oh, it's beautiful."

"It's made from volcanic rock. There are two active volcanos in Sicily, did you know?" I shook my head. "I thought it would go just lovely with your dark hair."

I placed the necklace around my neck.

"See? Beautiful." She smiled at me.

A waiter, who looked about thirteen, dressed in the same outfit as the host, materialized at our table, holding pad and pen in hand. "Can I get you drinks?"

"Vodka tonic, light on the ice," Meredith instructed without hesitation.

My eyes widened. It was only four o'clock in the afternoon. I didn't remember Meredith as much of a drinker.

"Are you joining me?"

"Oh, I . . . sure. Vodka tonic for me, too, please."

I might need a dash of Dutch courage to get through this conversation—or since it was vodka, it should be called "Russian courage" instead? Whatever it was, I bet I needed it.

The waiter left to collect our drinks, and I decided there was no point delaying the inevitable. As I'd just discovered, thanks to Paige,

Meredith knew I'd started dating again. I was certain she wasn't happy about it. It may be almost three years since Dan passed away, but that clearly wasn't long enough for her to come to terms with the idea I'd moved on.

I clasped my hands together under the table. "I know why you wanted to see me."

"You do?"

I nodded. "It's because Paige told you I've been dating someone new."

She nodded. "Yes, I'd heard that. Is he a nice man?"

I bit back the smile that always wanted to spread across my face when I thought of Ryan. He was more than nice. In fact, I was pretty darn sure he was the guy for me—my Last First Date.

I nodded.

"That's good, Bailey. I can see by the look on your face you have strong feelings for him."

I wrung my hands in my lap. "Meredith, I know this must be really hard for you, and I'm so sorry." My chest tightened as tears stung my eyes. Seeing Meredith brought Dan's loss screaming back. "You know I loved Daniel, I'll always love him. No man could ever take his place in my heart."

Her shoulders drooped, her lips forming a thin line.

My tears threatened to spill down my face. I sniffed, willing them not to.

"Oh, Bailey, sweetie. Here." She popped the clasp on her purse and pulled out a nicely pressed lace handkerchief. She handed it to me.

I shot her a watery smile and took it, dabbing the corners of my eyes. "Thank you, I don't know what came over me."

The waiter delivered our vodka tonics and I took a large gulp, and then another, hoping the alcohol would do its work.

"Do you know why I wanted to see you today?"

I nodded, looking down. "Dan."

"Oh, Bailey. Yes, it's about Daniel, but mainly it's about *you*."

I looked up into her eyes. "Me?"

"I wanted to tell you it's okay. When Paige and Josh told me you had met a man, I admit it stung at first. Daniel was meant to be the one you spent your life with, to make a home with."

I bit my lip, willing myself not to cry again.

"I know that can't be, and as his mother, there will always be a huge hole in my heart. I know it will never mend." She paused, and I could tell she was struggling to keep her grief in check. "You? You're young, you have your life ahead of you. Daniel would have wanted you to move on, to find someone worthy of you, worthy of your love."

Well, that was it. The floodgates were officially open. Here was my almost-mother-in-law, telling me she condoned me dating another man. It was heartbreaking and kind, and oh-so difficult to hear.

"Thank you," I managed, although with my stuffed-up nose and watery eyes it probably sounded more like "dangoo."

She reached across the table and squeezed my hand. As I looked up into her face, I could see her own eyes were wet.

"We will always love him, we will always miss him, no matter what. I can't have another son. I had two, and now I've only got Joshua. But you? Bailey, honey, it's been three years on the twenty-sixth since he passed away. Three years."

I nodded, my heart aching. A week after Cassie and Will's wedding, I'd be remembering what I could have had with Dan. In some ways, it felt like forever since he'd gone, in others, like it was just yesterday.

"You deserve to live more than a half-life, Bailey."

"Thank you," I managed. I regarded her through watery eyes. This woman, with the dead child, was telling me I was free to love again, to move on from her son.

My heart could have broken in two.

Chapter 18

"ARGH!" PAIGE SLAMMED THE phone down on the counter.

"The call didn't go well, I take it?" I asked, my brows raised.

"That Eddie Whatshisface is virtually taking over all the catering business out there! We've only got another couple of small events since I fixed the problem on our website."

"Really? What about the party for Susannah West? We were the front runner for that one, right?"

Paige pressed her lips into a line and shook her head. "Stolen, right from under our noses."

I hung my Cozy Cottage apron up on a hook by the back door and turned to face her. "You're telling me that other than Cassie and Will's wedding next month and a handful of new clients, we've lost every booking to Devour?"

She nodded, her lips tight. "Yup. Oh, I am so annoyed!"

"But I'm sure things will pick up, now that you've fixed the website and we're no longer handing our potential clients to Devour on a platter. If you'll excuse the pun."

Paige hung her head. "I'm such an idiot."

I wasn't going to argue with her, but there was no point in dwelling on it. "Paige, you've fixed it now, and what's done is done."

I tapped my finger against my chin, an idea percolating. "You know what? I think we should meet him, this Eddie guy. Not as us, of course. We could give him a fake name, make up some event we're holding."

Paige knitted her brows together. "Why?"

"So we can look him in the eye, get the measure of the man, as my nona would have said."

Paige's face lit up. "Oh, yes. And tell him to stop undercutting us all the time and stealing all our business."

I laughed. "Maybe we might want to be a little more subtle about it than that, honey. We could just arrange to meet him to get some more info on them."

"I like the way you're thinking, *Ms*. Bond."

"Well, I'm hardly a spy. Just a woman who wants to protect her business."

Paige pushed a few keys on her laptop. She picked up the phone where she had unceremoniously slammed it before and handed it to me. "You do the honors."

"It would be my pleasure."

She called out the number, and I dialed. It rang a couple of times before it went to answerphone. "Yes, hello," I began, affecting my best posh British accent. "My name is . . . Claire Fraser."

Paige had to stifle a laugh as I named the heroine in *Outlander*, a box set we'd watched together a couple of weeks ago on a particularly wet and gray Sunday.

"I'm looking for a caterer for a party I'm holding next month. It's dinner for—" Paige mouthed one hundred, but I decided to amp it up a notch. "Five hundred."

I wanted him to *really* want this.

"Please call me as soon as you can. Much appreciated."

I left my personal cell phone number and hung up before Paige's laughter came tumbling out.

"You sounded like the Queen of freaking England!"

"Do you think I was convincing?"

"Totally."

"Well, now we just need to sit back and wait to hear from this slime-ball called Eddie Smith who's been stealing all our customers."

WE DIDN'T HAVE to wait long.

Later that evening, I was applying the finishing touches to my mascara, getting ready to meet Ryan, Josh, and Paige at O'Dowd's for a "thank goodness the week is over" Saturday evening drink. My phone rang on the bathroom counter beside me.

The ring tone pulled me out of my head, where I'd been lost, thinking about Ryan. You see, tonight was our first date since my conversation with Meredith. Although she'd given me her blessing to date him, seeing her had unsettled me. Sure, Ryan and I had been texting, and I saw him when he came in to get a coffee at the café on Thursday.

But something had changed for me.

Gone was that almost euphoric feeling I'd first had at the ball, that certainty there could be something big between us. It was replaced by . . . doubt.

Although Meredith had made it clear she supported me seeing someone new, I was finding it difficult to allow myself to let go of the feeling I was doing something wrong. There was something in her face, something that contradicted her words.

Something that made me know beyond a whisper of a doubt that seeing Ryan was disloyal to Dan's memory.

I tried to push it all from my mind as I slotted the mascara wand back into its case and screwed it in place. I picked up my phone. "Hello?"

"Hello, is that Ms. Fraser?" a female voice said on the other end of the line.

I almost told her she had the wrong number, but caught myself in time. "Yes, this is Claire Fraser."

Paige would be so proud of my regal British accent.

"Wonderful. This is Siobhan from Devour Catering. We received your voicemail regarding a dinner for five hundred?"

"Yes. My husband, Jamie, and I are celebrating our anniversary." Another *Outlander* character, the sexy Scottish hero.

"How wonderful."

Lucky for me, Siobhan clearly didn't watch the show.

"Yes. We want an intimate dinner with some of our closest friends."

That's right; all five hundred of them.

"How exciting. We would love to have the opportunity to cater that for you. What date is that?"

I gave her a date about seven weeks from now, figuring that was far enough away for it to be believable.

"I'll arrange for Fiona Whitefield, one of our catering coordinators, to meet with you to discuss our options, pricing, and other points. Does that sound good?"

"Oh, I thought I would be meeting with Eddie Smith. I've heard such truly marvelous things about him."

Like he's trying to destroy Cozy Cottage Catering.

I knew I was hamming it up, but the whole point of this charade was to get to meet him, to look him square in the eyes, as I'd told Paige.

"Mr. Smith is super busy right now, but Fiona could meet you early next week?"

"Well, I don't want to deal with anyone else. No offense to Fiona."

"I see. Could you hold the line for a moment, please?"

"Of course."

She must have put her hand over the receiver. I could hear muffled talking as I waited. I applied my lipstick, still holding the phone to my ear.

"Ms. Fraser? Eddie Smith would be happy to meet with you. Would Monday work for you?"

"Perfect." We arranged a time for me to meet the famous Eddie Smith, and I hung up. I gazed at my reflection in the bathroom mirror, a nefarious smile forming on my face.

Game on.

"YOU'VE GOT BALLS, did you know that?" Ryan's arm was wrapped around my shoulders, and he gave me a squeeze.

I flashed him a smile and tried not to tense up. Before my conversation with Meredith, this would have felt perfectly normal. We were dating, after all, and had been for a while now.

But that was before—before I started to feel the way I do, before Dan's memory had come back to haunt me.

"I hope she doesn't actually *have* balls." Josh was sitting across the table from us. "That would be bad news for you, dude."

I laughed, trying to loosen up. "It's no big deal. I just put on a fake accent and made up a fake event. That's all."

"Yeah, but you're going to do it in person on Monday," Josh replied.

I bit my lip. He had a point. It was one thing to pretend I was someone else over the phone, quite another to do it in front of the guy—even if we had good reason to do so.

"I'll be there, too," Paige said. "Although I'm not sure I can do the whole fake accent thing."

"I bet you can. Go on, give it a shot." Ryan smiled at her.

Paige shook her head.

"Come on, babe. Who knows? You might be amazing at it." Josh winked at her and she shook her head some more, her grin as wide as a Cheshire cat's.

My belly twisted at the sight of them. They were so obviously in love with one another. It was an uncomplicated love, straightforward, easy.

I glanced at Ryan, who smiled back at me. I chewed the inside of my lip, wishing I didn't feel this way, wishing things could go back to the way they were before I saw Meredith.

Before I got stuck in my head.

"Okay. Here goes." Paige shook her shoulders out and lifted her chin. She cleared her throat. "Good evening. I'm Lady Crawley, and I demand you show me to your stables. I simply must see the horses."

I tried not to laugh, but it was a truly terrible accent.

"Honey, what was *that*?" Josh's eyes danced, his grin broad.

"It sounded Irish and Kiwi and somehow almost like you were from New York,' Ryan said.

"I was being English." Paige looked affronted.

"Lady Crawley from *Downton Abbey*, right?" I said, and she nodded. "You men wouldn't get it."

"Chick show?" Ryan asked.

I cocked my head. "Both men and women have enjoyed *Downton Abbey*, thank you, Ryan." I was pretending to be offended, although I was pretty sure the TV show's primary audience was more than likely female.

"Is it set somewhere between New York, New Zealand, and Ireland?" Josh had a cheeky glint in his eye.

When Paige crossed her arms, clearly not enjoying where the conversation had gone, he wrapped his arm around her and kissed her forehead. "Paige, you have so many qualities. It wouldn't be fair on the rest of us if you could do great accents, too."

That seemed to do the trick, and Paige loosened up immediately.

See? Uncomplicated love.

"Anyway, Paige and I are meeting this Eddie Smith guy at The Royal on Monday after we close up the Cozy Cottage for the day," I said, naming one of the swankier hotels in Auckland.

"The Royal is very appropriate for the Queen," Ryan said. "Just be careful, okay? You've got no idea who this guy is. And if he really has been targeting you, things could get tricky once he sees you."

I smiled at him. Although it felt good to have a man looking out for me once more, I couldn't shake this feeling. This feeling that something was wrong.

This feeling that I shouldn't be with Ryan.

"More drinks?" I needed a breather, to try to get my head together. I knew Ryan was a great guy, and we'd had so much fun together over the last few weeks. I'd started to develop some real feelings toward him, feelings beyond simply being attracted to his Thor-like good looks and flirty charm.

Real feelings, deep feelings.

This thing between us was going somewhere, somewhere big. I couldn't let my sense of disloyalty toward Dan stop me from finding happiness.

Paige, Ryan, and Josh gave me their orders, and I walked over to the bar. I'd only just ordered the drinks when I felt a hand on my arm. I turned and smiled at Josh.

"I thought you could use some help."

"It's only three drinks. I'm pretty sure this waitress can handle it." I pointed my thumb at myself.

"Yeah, I know you can. I guess I just wanted to talk to you, just you. I know Mum came to see you."

My hairs lifted on the back of my neck at the mention of Meredith. "Yes, she did."

"I'm really glad. She cares for you a lot, you know."

I nodded, trying not to think of the look on her face, the way in which her words were at odds with her pained expression.

"We both think it's awesome you've met someone new. Ryan's a good guy."

"Yeah, thanks."

The bartender placed the drinks on the bar in front of us, and I handed over some cash. "Can you bring the last one?" I nodded at Ryan's bottle of beer.

"See? You did need me." Josh winked at me and we returned to the table.

No sooner had we sat down, when Nash, Marissa's boyfriend, came over and stood at our table, grinning at us. "Hey there, party people."

"Hey, Nash," I said as everyone else greeted him. "Are you here with Marissa?"

"I sure am. We're having a drink before dinner with some of her work colleagues."

"Do you want to join us?" Josh offered. "If you're happy hanging out with your kid sister on a Saturday night, that is," he added, looking at Ryan.

"I've done it too many times to be bothered by it now." Ryan shrugged.

"Cool. Be right back."

I glanced over at the bar where Nash joined Marissa, who was ordering their drinks. I could see Nash talking with her, and she turned then smiled and waved at us.

I waved back. The last time I'd seen Marissa, she was warning me off her brother once more. I wondered how she'd react to seeing us together tonight?

Josh and Ryan pulled up a couple more chairs, and a moment later, Marissa and Nash joined us.

Marissa took a seat between Paige and me. "This is a cozy double date." She shot me a look.

My insides twisted. Marissa had left me a voicemail, asking when we could meet to talk again. I'd meant to get back to her, but seeing Meredith had thrown me, and I'd pushed it to the back of my mind.

"It's a triple date, now," Paige replied.

"I guess it is."

I chewed the inside of my lip, not sure what to do. In the end, Marissa made the decision for me.

"Can we go talk?" Her voice was quiet enough only I could hear.

"Sure. Ladies?"

"Good call."

We excused ourselves from the table and headed across the floor. For once, I was thankful women had the reputation of always going in packs to the bathroom.

Once inside, the door closed behind us, Marissa launched straight into it. "We didn't get the chance to finish that conversation."

"No, I . . . I've been busy. And anyway, you've already told me Ryan's too messed up right now. It's sweet you're worried about your brother, really it is."

Marissa's mouth twisted. "It's not him I'm worried about."

"It's not?"

She shook her head. "It's you, Bailey."

I knitted my brows together. "Why would you be worried about me?"

She exhaled. "I found out he went to see Amelia, his ex."

"He did?"

"I asked him about it, but he wouldn't tell me what they talked about. Bailey, I wanted to tell you so you didn't get hurt. I know you've been through a lot."

My mind began to whirr. Ryan hadn't said anything to me about seeing Amelia, and he'd made that speech at the ball about not wanting me to be a rebound girl. It had been convincing, honest. At least I'd thought it had been. We'd been seeing each other for weeks since then.

I opened my mouth to speak, but nothing came out. Of course, him going to see her could be entirely innocent. They could be meeting to get final closure, to decide they could be friends, maybe even to return an old T-shirt or something?

But then again, it could be less than innocent, too.

"Bailey, I'm so sorry to have to tell you this. I just thought you should know."

"No, no. It's fine. Really." I pressed my lips together, fighting the sudden and overwhelming urge to cry. Ryan was the first man I'd let myself fall for since Dan, the first man I'd thought I could have a future with. It had been a long time, and I trusted him.

Or at least, I had.

"Do. . . do you think they're going to get back together?" I didn't know if I wanted to hear the answer.

Marissa shrugged. "I've no idea. All I know is I saw them at that café downtown, Alessandro's. Do you know it?"

I nodded.

"They looked, I don't know, comfortable together. Amelia was bad news for Ryan. She kinda chewed him up and spat him out. It took him a long time to get over her."

"I know."

Ryan had told me about how she'd broken up with him, how he

had thought she was the woman he was going to spend the rest of his life with.

I knew first-hand how hard it was to get over a love you've had and lost.

"I asked him about it afterwards, and he told me it was none of my business."

"Oh. Right."

"I'm sorry." Marissa rubbed my arm. "You thought he was your Last First Date, didn't you?"

I nodded, my chest tightening. "I understand the need to go back. He was deeply in love with her. Believe me, I totally get that."

And I knew if I could get a second chance with Dan, I'd grab it with both hands, too.

Chapter 19

ON MONDAY AFTERNOON, PAIGE and I waited at The Royal Hotel, ready to meet the infamous Eddie Smith. We were wound up, both reminding one another to stick with the story we were Claire Fraser and her friend, Bree, looking for a caterer for a large party.

Considering my inner turmoil about Ryan, it was a tall order, that was for sure.

After Marissa's revelation about Amelia, I'd told everyone I had a headache and went home. Of course, being the gentleman he was—maybe a cheating gentleman still in love with his ex, but a gentleman all the same—Ryan insisted on seeing me home. I made up some story about thinking I may be contagious, so once he'd seen me inside, he left.

I spent the next thirty-six hours wrestling with not only what Marissa had said about him seeing Amelia, but trying to work out what I wanted, what felt right to me.

The jury was still out.

I noticed Paige clenching her hands in her lap.

"Don't be nervous. We got this."

"I'm nervous as all heck. It's my fault he got our list of contacts, so I'm totally responsible."

I couldn't argue with that.

"Plus, I've never done anything like this before."

"You mean you've never gone undercover to catch a bad guy stealing our customers at a swanky hotel in downtown Auckland?"

She let out a laugh. "Funnily enough, no. Although I now wish you'd agreed to letting Ryan come along."

As I said, Ryan was a gentleman. He didn't want Paige and me doing what we're doing now, and he got all manly and protective about it all. I told him we'd put on our big girl panties and manage just fine.

And here we were, on our own, managing just fine—big girl panties firmly in place.

"Okay. I've been thinking, and here's how I think we should play it," I said. "I think we drop the whole pretense of having a party and instead just ask him why he's been targeting us."

"Just come out with it?"

"Unless you have a better idea?"

Paige shook her head. "I guess not." She picked up her tea cup to take a sip, a pensive look on her face.

"Good." I glanced at my watch, my own nerves clanging around my body. I wasn't big on confrontation, preferring instead to smooth things over, to try to find some middle ground everyone could be happy with. But this was about our new business and being held back from even being given a shot at it. We needed to do this.

Paige lowered her cup with a *clank* onto her saucer. "Oh, my God."

I shot her a look. She'd gone pale, her eyes focused on something across the room behind me.

"What is it?"

"You are not going to believe this."

"What?" I turned to see what had her jaw dropping. My own followed suit the moment my eyes clapped on him.

It was Fake Jamie.

Heading our way.

I turned back to face Paige, hoping he hadn't seen us—knowing he probably had.

My heart banged against my ribs, and I scrunched my eyes shut. In an instant, I was back in the hallway at the Cozy Cottage with Fake Jamie breathing down my neck, his grip firm, painful on my arm. My hands began to sweat.

"What is he doing here?" Paige hissed.

"I don't know."

"Well, I can tell you one thing for certain, I'm going to give him a piece of my mind if he comes anywhere near you."

"Maybe he hasn't seen us? Maybe he's going to walk straight passed us?" My voice was breathless, shaking.

Paige looked up, and I could sense he'd come to a stop behind me. "Maybe not."

"Hello, ladies. Is one of you Claire Fraser?"

What the . . .?

Before I had the chance to pick my jaw up off the floor, Paige pushed herself up. "I am."

"Pleased to meet you. I'm Eddie Smith, from Devour Catering. I understand you wanted to meet me personally."

Paige's eyes almost popped out of her head. "*You're* Eddie Smith?"

"Yeah, I get that a lot."

Just as smarmy and cocky as he was on our speed date.

I closed my eyes, wishing I were anywhere but here. Harry Potter's invisibility cloak would come in handy right about now.

Instead, I forced myself to stand up on trembling legs, turn and face him. I clenched my fists at my side.

Eddie's eyes landed on me and recognition breezed across his face. "You."

I locked my jaw and glared at him. "Yes, me."

"You're friends with Claire?"

I shook my head, wishing my glare could pierce him, right where it hurt.

"Well, Claire and I have got some party planning to do. Five hundred guests, actually."

"Ah, no we don't." Paige shook her head.

His eyes darted from Paige to me and back again. Comprehension appeared on his face. "There's no party, is there?"

I shook my head.

His eyes swept over us, appraising us in that creepy way he'd perfected. "Oh, I get it. You two clever little girls thought you could make up some fake party to get me here." He smiled at me, flicking his Bee Gees hair. "You didn't have to make something up to see me, you know. I'd be happy to take you out, show you a good time, babe."

Seriously, I could have vomited on the spot.

"I don't want to go out with you now or at any time. I just wanted to look the person in the eye who's been taking all our customers, undercutting us at every turn."

He didn't even flinch. "Well, you've met him."

"Why do it? We're just a small start-up, trying to get a business off the ground," Paige said.

Eddie looked at me, raising his chin. "She knows."

My pulse sped up, my body tensing. I could barely believe what he'd just said. "You're doing this to get back at me because I *rejected* you?"

The self-satisfied look in his eyes told me everything I needed to know. "Is it working?"

I gripped the chair that had been my barricade, and pushed it aside, stepping closer to him. "Of all the idiotic, childish, petty reasons to try to hurt someone, that has got to be the lowest."

"Calm down, babe. All's fair in love and war."

"Don't call me that. I'm not your babe."

"Everything all right here?" It was a voice from behind me.

I turned to see Ryan, his eyes focused on me.

I blinked at him. "Wh-what are you doing here?"

"I see you brought your guard dog," Eddie spat.

"Bailey, are you okay?"

My nostrils flared as my eyes slid from Ryan to Eddie. He shot me another one of his slimy, smug looks, only this time it was tinged with something else. This time, it was tinged with triumph.

He'd won. And he darn well knew it.

Ryan's hand touched mine, sending a jolt of electricity through me, waking me up. I took a sudden step back, bumping into the table, the cups and saucers rattling. "What are you doing here?"

"I wanted to make sure you were safe."

I ground my teeth. "I'm fine. I just . . . I need to go."

I grabbed my purse, my chest tight, my limbs trembling. I needed to get out of here, I needed to get far away. Fake Jamie and his campaign to destroy our business, Ryan turning up here after I'd made it clear I didn't want him to.

My guilt over Daniel.

All of it, all mixed up inside, ready to explode out of me like a volcano on the brink.

I slung my purse over my shoulder and pushed past Ryan.

"Bailey, wait!" Paige called out.

I didn't stop, I didn't look back.

I dashed across the marble floor and pushed my way through the revolving door. I stepped out into the dull, cloudy afternoon light, the sidewalk bustling with people going about their business. I paused, trying to remember where I'd left my car, my brain like scrambled eggs.

"Bailey, what's going on?"

I looked up into Ryan's eyes. He was gazing down at me, a cloud of concern across his face.

"I can't do it. I can't." I tried to blink back the tears that threatened my eyes, but they slid down my cheeks. I wiped them furiously away with the back of my hand.

"You can't do what, exactly? Because if it's dealing with that jerk in there, I'd happily do it for you."

I shook my head, a lump the size of Texas in my throat. "I can't do this. With you."

"Why?" The pain in his voice was clear.

"You know why. You're still in love with her. And I . . ."

What was I? Scared? Confused?

All of the above?

"Amelia? Are you *insane*? I'm not in love with her. Where the hell did you get that idea?"

I stood my ground. I wasn't going to be second best to some other woman. Although I knew this was about more than just Amelia. "You went to see her. Admit it. You're still in love with her."

He put his hands on my arms. My body stiffened at his touch. "Bailey, don't you know I'm in love with you?"

In an instant, the air was sucked out of my lungs. My hand flew to my chest, as the world began to spin around me.

I shook my head, my throat dry as I pulled away from him. "No. No, you're not."

Ryan smiled, stepping in closer to me. "I am. Bailey De Luca, I am one hundred percent in love with you."

"Don't say that. Please." I bit my lip, fresh tears streaming down my face.

"It's the truth, pure and simple. How can I not be? Amelia is in the past, over. It's you, Bailey. It's you."

"No." I shook my head, panic rising inside.

And then I turned and ran.

I almost crashed into a man in a suit in my need to get away. Apologizing, I stumbled past him and dashed down the street, going as fast as my heels could take me.

I didn't look back.

And all I could think about was the last man who said he'd loved me.

The man I'd lost.

Chapter 20

I ARRIVED AT WORK on Monday morning exhausted, the bags under my eyes large enough to carry the belongings of an entire family on vacation to Fiji. Since that fateful day at The Royal Hotel, I'd hardly slept a wink, instead lying on my back, staring up at the ceiling, trying to make sense of . . . well, everything.

Starting with Fake Jamie slash Fabio slash Eddie Smith. *Whatever* his name was. Never in my life had I been victimized by someone the way he had victimized me. Sure, I'd had girls be mean to me at high school, a couple even moving my desk away from theirs or throwing all my school work in the trash. That was harsh at the time, but it was just fourteen-year-olds being catty and nasty.

This? This was a whole different league.

Out of sheer bitterness, Eddie had set out to ruin Cozy Cottage Catering. And he'd done a darn good job of it. All because I rejected him.

So much for "hell hath no fury like a woman scorned." This man's fury was off the freaking charts.

And then, of course, my mind kept bouncing back to Ryan. Turning up at The Royal Hotel when I'd asked him not to was one thing, but I knew there was something deeper that was bothering me, something I was finding hard to face.

When he'd said he loved me, with that look in his eye, it had catapulted me right back to when Dan was alive, right back to when he'd first uttered those three little words to me. To when I'd said them back to him. And I'd had unquestioning faith in that love, I thought it'd be forever. I thought our love could survive anything.

How wrong I had been.

No one had touched my heart the way Ryan had. No one other than Dan. How could I have such deep, strong feelings for Ryan when I'd already given my heart away to another?

It simply wasn't mine to give anymore.

Although my head knew Dan was gone, my heart didn't. And there was no room for anyone else while he was still there.

I wasn't ready to say a final goodbye. Not now, not ever.

I let out a heavy sigh as I tied my Cozy Cottage apron around my waist, my heart settling at the bottom of my belly. I had a business to run, and despite the catering company looking like it was dead in the water, we had a wedding to prepare for Cassie and Will.

I breathed in the delicious scent as I pulled a freshly baked flourless chocolate and raspberry cake out of the oven. I glanced up as Paige came through the back door. Her features creased up in concern as her eyes landed on mine.

"Bailey, thank goodness. I've called and called."

"Yeah, sorry about that. I needed some time."

I'd switched my phone off to avoid having to face Ryan—and everyone else. It had worked. Shame I couldn't have switched my mind off, too.

She placed her purse on the kitchen counter. "I get it. He's a creep, and what he did to you is horrible."

I nodded, placing the cake on a wire rack on the counter. "I know."

She walked around the edge of the counter until she was standing in front of me. "He's a vindictive idiot, not worth your time."

I nodded again. Yes, the way Eddie had targeted our business was beyond terrible, and he deserved to be punished in cruel and unusual ways.

But it wasn't him who had me in knots.

"And Ryan and you? Is everything okay there? By the time I paid the check and stepped outside, you had already taken off."

I looked down at the floor. "There is no Ryan and me. Not anymore."

"There's not?" Paige couldn't keep the shock from her voice. "I thought you two were great. I thought he was your Last First Date."

I shook my head, my chest aching, my eyelids hot.

"What happened?"

How could I explain that Ryan didn't stand a chance, that he could *never* stand a chance?—not against Dan.

I had to admit it to myself. I was in love with a ghost.

"I don't know. We weren't right, I guess." I lifted my head, plastering on a smile. "Hey, we're presenting the final menu to Cassie and Will tonight, right? I'm excited about that."

The look on her face told me she knew I was deliberately changing the subject. She was generous enough to let me have it. "I am, too. I think they're going to love it. And it's not far away now."

"No, less than a month."

She paused, running her fingers over the counter. "Hey, speaking of our catering business."

I shook my head. "I've lost the heart for it."

She nodded. "I thought as much. But I don't think we should make any hasty decisions right now. Let's just put it on ice, 'kay?"

"Okay."

She stepped over to me and pulled me in for a hug. I gave her a quick squeeze and then moved away before the tears began to pool in my eyes. I could deal with the emotional soap opera my life had become, but not in the face of her kindness.

And I'd had more than enough of crying for today.

I concentrated on loosening the cake out of its tin. "Can you please get that carrot cake in the oven?" I nodded at the counter where I'd placed the batter in a cake tin. I was awake so early, I'd gotten to the café in the middle of the night and had set about baking.

I'd always loved to bake. It was kind of my therapy. When things went wrong, I would pull out one of Nona's recipes and whip something up, the process of measuring and mixing, the satisfaction of baking something delicious, working to calm me.

This morning I'd baked a *Cassata alla Siciliana*, an orange and almond syrup cake, the chocolate and raspberry cake I'd just turned out, and had a carrot cake ready for me to ice later with cream cheese frosting.

Four cakes, but still I hadn't been able to find any peace.

"I've started in on the wedding cake, by the way."

"You have? I didn't think we'd do anything until next week."

"Oh, I had time this morning." Like three hours. "I've worked out how much of each of the ingredients we'll need, based on the size and design we've agreed on with them. Now all we have to do is bake it, ice it, decorate it, and voila."

"Is that all?" Paige laughed.

We were using a fruit cake recipe Nona had used to make for my cousin's wedding some years ago. She had baked it weeks before, storing it in an airtight container and "feeding" it every week to keep it moist. We had discussed doing the same, and with the wedding less than a month away now, we planned to begin baking this week.

I glanced at the clock on the wall. "It's almost opening time. Is Sophie due in?"

"She sure is."

"Would it be okay with you if I hung out in the back here and got on with baking the wedding cake?"

Sleep-deprivation and emotional turmoil weren't a great combination when dealing with customers. Hiding away in the kitchen for the day seemed like a much better option for me.

"Honey, you've got to do what works for you. Soph and I will be just fine."

There was a knock on the back door, and Paige wiped her hands as she walked over to answer it. "I bet that's Josh delivering the coffee beans. He's early today, though."

She pulled the door open. "Oh."

It wasn't Josh.

"Hey, Ryan," Paige said.

"Can I talk to Bailey, please, Paige?" His voice was quiet, controlled.

Paige held the door open and glanced over at me, her face once again creased up in concern. "Bailey?"

I swallowed, my eyes meeting Ryan's, my chest tightening. I gave a brief nod. I had to end this properly.

I had to let him go.

I rinsed my hands and dried them off, giving myself a moment to steady my nerves. I'd been dodging his calls, I knew this time would come. And he deserved to hear from me, even if he wouldn't want to hear what I had to say.

Out in the alley behind the café, I looked down at his feet, searching for the words.

"Bailey, what happened? I thought we were good." His voice was full of hurt, full of unexpressed grief. It twisted my heart to know I was the cause, that I'd done this to him.

I looked up and into his sad hazel eyes, my breath catching in my throat as I took in the pain written plainly across his face. He looked achingly handsome in his open-neck powder blue shirt, his dirty blonde hair messy.

"I'm sorry." My hand on my chest, I tried to hold my pain in. My breath shortened. "I just can't. Please understand. I thought I could, but I can't."

He placed a warm hand on my bare arm. I shivered at his touch, my heart heavy.

"Why? You've got to tell me why. Bailey, you owe me that much."

Dan had been gone for three years on the twenty-sixth. By developing feelings for Ryan—serious "this could turn into love" types of feelings—meant Dan was really gone.

Not ever coming back.

How could I tell Ryan that?

He stepped closer to me and placed his other hand on my arm. I could smell his cologne and felt my legs weaken.

"We can work this out. I love you, Bailey, and I think you love me, too."

I swallowed, that knife turning inside. I looked up and steeled myself. "I . . . I'm sorry, but I just don't feel the same."

I held my breath as he studied my face, his brows knitted together.

"I don't believe you." His voice was harsh, cutting through me.

"It's the truth. Now, I really have to get back inside. I'll . . . um, I'll see you 'round."

He dropped his hands from my arms and I turned away from him. I took a tentative step toward the door, my vision blurred, my heart thudding against my ribs. I fumbled for the door knob, grasping onto it. As I pushed the door open and stumbled inside, I didn't look back.

I couldn't.

I didn't want to see the pain on his face, knowing I'd caused it. It would be just too much to bear.

Chapter 21

IT WAS THE MORNING of Cassie and Will's wedding, and Cassie and we three bridesmaids were getting ready in a suite at The Windsor Inn. It was a former stately home that had been made into a hotel and wedding venue, with its English country garden charm and beautiful setting. Their wedding was to be held outside on the rolling lawn in a perfectly romantic setting, followed by a reception in a large, elegantly decorated marquee.

Today, however, it wasn't looking set to be quite so perfectly romantic.

It was raining. No, scratch that—it was pouring. Monsoon-like. And it didn't show signs of stopping any time soon.

"Go away, rain!" Cassie stood in a fluffy white hotel robe, her arms crossed, glaring out the window at the dark rain clouds.

"I'm not sure that approach is going to work, Cassie," Marissa said from her comfy chair by the coffee table, laden with tubes of makeup.

"Don't worry. Rain is good luck on your wedding day, right, Bailey?" Paige sat in a dining chair, looking up at the ceiling as the makeup artist applied eyeliner to her lower lids.

I had no clue whether rain was good luck or bad luck or any

type of luck on a wedding day, but Cassie didn't need to hear that. "Totally good luck."

"It's meant to get worse before it gets better," Justine, the makeup artist, announced. "I heard it on the radio on my way here. Rain, gale force winds, thunder and lightning. The works."

She so wasn't helping.

Cassie groaned. "Are you freaking kidding me?" She plunked herself down on the sofa, her bottom lip protruding. "This wedding is a disaster!"

"No, it's not. I'm sure the hotel has back-up options for this sort of thing," Paige said, her gaze still on the ceiling.

"Exactly," I echoed. "This is Auckland. Four seasons in one day, right?"

Cassie shrugged, tugging at the soft waves the hairdresser had perfected only an hour before. "I guess."

"We just have to wait and see what happens with the rain. The wedding's not for another three hours, anyway," Marissa said from her spot on the sofa. "If it's got to be somewhere else, then it's got to be somewhere else."

Marissa was ever the pragmatist.

There was a loud rap on the door.

"I'll get it." I sprang up from my seat, padded across the plush-carpeted floor, and pulled the door open.

Tania, the wedding coordinator, in her sensible gray pantsuit and tight bun, bustled past me and into the suite, a worried look on her face. "Ladies. Things are not looking good out there."

Cassie wrapped her arms around her body. "Tell me something we don't know, Tania."

"Well, the All Blacks team has just been announced for the summer tour." Tania's eyes darted around us all.

And . . . *crickets.*

Tania laughed. "You asked me to tell you something you didn't know. Sorry, silly joke. Trying to lighten the mood. And I am a big rugby fan."

"Good to know." Marissa shot me a look.

Cassie simply blinked at her. I could only imagine what was running through her mind right about now.

"So. Here's the deal. The hotel can rearrange the marquee to accommodate the wedding service. They just need to get the go-ahead from you and Will. I've just been to see the guys. Will was, ah, still getting dressed." She grinned, blushing. "He was in his boxers, actually. Does he work out?"

My brows sprung up. First a joke about rugby and now she was lusting after the groom? Where did Cassie and Will find this wedding planner?

Cassie ignored the question. I mean, how would you respond to that, anyway? "What did Will want to do about the ceremony?"

As if by cosmic coincidence, Cassie's phone on the coffee table began to ring. I picked it up and glanced at the screen. "It's Will."

She walked over to me, her brows knitted together as she regarded the phone. "I know it's bad luck to see the groom on the day of your wedding, but is it bad luck to talk to him, too?"

"I don't think that's a thing." Marissa shook her head.

"Definitely not a thing," Tania confirmed—although I'm not sure anyone was listening to a word she had to say after her previous comments.

Paige and I both agreed, and the makeup artist shrugged, pleading ignorance of such things.

Wise move.

"I'm gonna answer it." Cassie took the phone from me and swiped to answer. "Hey, honey."

We all watched as she paced the room, listening to whatever it was her soon-to-be husband was saying. "Right . . . okay . . . I know, it sucks . . . damn rain . . . I love you, too."

"Well?" I was as impatient as everyone else in the room to know what he'd said.

"He's not thrilled about it, but having the ceremony in the marquee looks like it's our only option." She slumped down on the sofa next to me, staring into space. "It's not going to be the way we envisioned it."

"Oh, Cassie. It'll still be wonderful." I rubbed her arm.

"Totally. And the rain will only add to the drama." Paige smiled at Cassie, her makeup complete.

"Wise choice," Tania said. "I'll go and get onto organizing it. You stay here, relaxed, getting ready. I'll check back in later. I might drop by the guys once more. You know, to see if everything's okay with them."

She bustled out of the room and closed the door behind herself.

"Where did you find that one?" Marissa asked Cassie. "A Justin Bieber concert? She's got to be about thirteen."

"At least we know she's a big rugby fan," I added with a smile.

Cassie let out a sigh. "She's Will's distant cousin by marriage. Someone's married to someone, and she's their daughter. Something like that. It's kinda complicated. She's not done a wedding before, and we said we'd let her plan ours so she got some experience for her C.V."

"She hasn't done a wedding before? You don't say." Marissa's voice dripped with sarcasm.

"She's been fine. I've really been doing most of the work. She's kind of been tagging along for the ride, more than anything."

"Well, as long as she doesn't need to be back for study hall," Marissa said with a laugh.

"Not helping." Cassie glared at her.

"Right, you're next." Justine pointed at Marissa. Paige stood up and Justine patted the empty seat.

She'd done my makeup straight after Cassie's so I could be ready to greet our catering staff when they arrived. Jason—of the "I'm Dan's doppelgänger" fame—was scheduled with a few of others, and Sophie had stepped up to help us out as well. Plus, we had hired some chefs to prepare the food we couldn't do beforehand. It was more than a little challenging to be a supportive and present part of the bridal party and run the catering at the same time. But Paige and I adored Cassie and Will and wanted to do whatever we could to make their day as special as it could be.

Paige moved over to the window, and Marissa took her seat.

My phone beeped in my pocket. I pulled it out to see who it was. Ryan's name flashed on the screen.

I'll keep my distance today, you don't have to worry.

My throat tightened. I hadn't seen or heard from Ryan since that early morning in the alley outside the café. He'd respected my need for distance, and I was grateful to him.

But no matter how I'd tried, I hadn't been able to get him out of my head—or my heart.

My guilt over Dan had reached Biblical proportions.

Ryan was one of the wedding guests, so even if I wanted to avoid him, that wasn't going to happen today. I'd heard he and Will had become golfing buddies, and Cassie had known him for years.

I typed out a message, pausing before I hit send.

You don't need to do that.

My thumb hovered over the "send" button. Instead of pressing it, I deleted the sentence and re-typed.

Thanks.

My phone made that whooshing sound as the text was sent. I held it against my tummy, surprised when it beeped once more. I turned the screen over to look at the message, half hoping it was Ryan, changing his mind, telling me he wasn't going to keep his distance.

Telling me he knew we were meant to be together.

It wasn't from Ryan. It was from Meredith.

Everything's set. I'll see you on Saturday. 11am.

My chest tightened. Saturday was the twenty-sixth, three years since Dan had passed away.

Three years since my life had changed irrevocably.

Last year Meredith, Josh, and I, along with Dan's father, George, commemorated Dan's short life by each releasing a balloon at the beach where we'd scattered his ashes. The beach he'd loved as a kid. This year we planned to do the same once more.

I sent a quick reply.

Thanks. See you then.

I turned my phone over and placed it on the coffee table. I knew Saturday would be incredibly hard, for me as well as for Dan's family. But it felt vital to do, vital not to forget him. Because we could never do that.

"Oh, my gosh. You guys!" Paige was standing at the window, her mouth dropped open as her eyes darted around the room.

"What is it?" Cassie's voice was tinged with panic.

"You've got to see. Come, quick."

Cassie, Marissa, Justine, and I rushed over to the large window.

I looked down to the lawn below. "What?"

Paige pointed over to the far corner of the lawn, where the marquee for the wedding was pitched, set against a line of elegant column trees. Only, instead of a large, elegant marquee capable of holding one-hundred and twenty guests, standing proud, white against the green grass, there was now a soggy, lumpy, white mess. One end was still upright, the other totally collapsed.

"The marquee's *fallen down*?" I uttered, barely believing my eyes.

It was official. This wedding was a disaster-in-the-making.

My mind instantly darted to the tables and the work Paige, Sophie, and I had put into setting them up early this morning. I heaved a sigh of relief that the food and the cake weren't due to be delivered for another hour or so.

"What are we going to do?" Cassie's face was aghast.

"Don't worry. We'll work something out, right, girls?" Paige's eyes flashed to mine.

"Totally." I sounded a gazillion percent more certain than I was. "We'll come up with something."

I looked at Paige and Marissa and mouthed "what?" They both shrugged, shaking their heads.

Cassie was still examining at the mess of the marquee on the lawn. She rubbed her neck, shaking her head. "I can't get married. I can't get married."

And then it hit me.

I gestured to Paige to follow me to the other side of the room, and we moved away from Cassie, leaving her with Marissa and Justine, all three still gazing at the shocking sight outside.

"Are you thinking what I'm thinking?" Paige said in hushed tones.

"If you're thinking we should have the wedding at the Cozy Cottage, then yes, totally."

Paige's face lit up, a smile forming on her pretty face. "You know what? I think Cassie would love that. The café has been such a big part of her life."

"It's not exactly the perfect romantic setting she was going for, but I'm not sure we have a lot of other options right now."

"Do you think we can fit one-hundred-and-fifty guests, though?"

I thought of our Cozy Cottage Jams and how we rearranged the tables to fit more people in. But it didn't come close to one-hundred-and-fifty.

Then, I remembered something I'd seen at Addison's old florist shop and a seed of an idea began to grow. "You know how there are those double wooden doors behind where we put the stage on a Friday night?"

Paige nodded. "I've always wondered about those."

"Well, they lead through to that florist shop that used to be next door, Addison's old place. She told me her shop and our café used to be a restaurant back in the day."

"And you're telling me this now why?"

"The shop is still up for sublease. I can contact Addi and ask her if we can rent it for the evening. It's got a beautiful courtyard out back, and we can open the doors from the café. It'll almost be like one big room."

Paige's face lit up. "That could actually work. Is it a covered courtyard?"

"Yup. The perfect place for a wedding ceremony." I grinned, thinking about the special feeling the courtyard had given me when Addi had shown it to me. "We'll need to organize more tables and chairs, but I think it could work."

Paige pulled me in for a quick hug. "Bailey, you're a genius."

"Well, I wouldn't go that far. Extremely intelligent, maybe?" I winked, and Paige laughed. "First thing I need to do before we say anything to Cassie is find out if we can rent that space."

"Do you know how to get hold of Addison?"

"Just leave it to me."

I collected my phone from the table and scrolled through my contacts. I knew Addi was in Florida, and I had no clue what time of day or night it was there, but this was an emergency. Although I didn't know her well, something told me she'd be happy to help us out.

The phone rang only a couple of times before she answered. "Bailey? Oh, my gosh. How are you?"

"I'm great, thanks. Look, we're in a bit of a jam here, and I was wondering if you could help us out?"

"Anything."

I explained what had happened and asked if we could use her old shop. She agreed in a heartbeat, insisting we have the place for free for the night and telling me where to collect the keys.

"That courtyard would be perfect for the ceremony," she said.

"I know, although it's not big enough to fit all the guests."

"Just as long as you have the bride and groom there, right?"

"Exactly."

I hung up from Addi and beamed at Paige. "We're on."

"Addison's a total life saver."

"I know, right? Remind me to bake her a huge cake next time she's back in New Zealand. Okay, let's think this through. The place has been closed all day, so you and I will need to get there with Sophie and the rest of the catering staff a-sap to set up."

Paige nodded. "I'll need to get on the phone right now to let them know. It's a good thirty-minute drive here from the city."

"Yes, good. I'll pack up my stuff and head straight back to the café to get things started."

"Aren't we forgetting one important detail?" Paige looked across the room at Cassie. She was still standing at the window, Marissa consoling her.

"Gotcha." I smiled. "One rather *important* detail."

We approached the window, excited we had the means to save the day.

"Cassie?" My voice was gentle.

She turned to look at us, her cheeks wet with tears.

I couldn't help the smile from bursting onto my face. "We've got an idea."

Chapter 22

"YOU WANT ME TO have my wedding at the Cozy Cottage?" Cassie's eyes were huge, her mouth forming an "o."

I glanced at Paige, suddenly not so sure our plan to save Cassie and Will's wedding would work. I mean, she would be going from a stately home in a stunning country setting to the café where she got her daily coffee and cake fix. She might well decide it wasn't nearly as classy or romantic as we thought.

"Yes?" I held my breath as Cassie blinked at me in disbelief.

She paused, pressing her lips together, her brows knitted. "I'll . . . I'll have to talk to Will."

"Of course, you do. This is both your and Will's wedding," Paige replied. "We thought you might like to have it at the café because it's been such an important place to you." She looked around the room. "To all of us, really."

"Not to me. I don't even know where it is," Justine said.

I erupted into a surprised laugh. "Okay, it's an important place to everyone but *you*."

"I can tell you one thing for sure, though—you won't be having your wedding in that tent out there," Justine continued.

I shot her a "not helping" look, and she shrugged.

We stood back to allow Cassie room to walk over to her phone. We watched as she collected it from the coffee table and punched in her passcode.

Cassie lifted the phone to her ear. She glanced at Paige and me, chewing on her lip. "Hey, Will . . . yes, I saw it . . . I know, it's a disaster . . . Tania's there? Are you fully dressed now? . . . Oh, no reason . . . Me too, but don't worry." She glanced back at Paige and me again, and the corners of her mouth twitched. "Me and the girls have got a plan . . . No, we're not going to get married at the driving range, Will." She rolled her eyes and mouthed "men" at us. "What do you think about getting married at the Cozy Cottage Café?" Her face broke into a grin, presumably at Will's reaction, her eyes flashing. "I thought you might say that."

I glanced at Paige. She smiled back at me, her eyes dancing.

"We're doing this?" I asked Cassie.

She nodded, her eyes filling with tears. The phone still at her ear, she said, "Hold on a sec."

She pressed her screen, and Will's voice boomed around the room. "Bailey? Paige?"

"Yes, we're here," Paige said.

"You two have saved the day. We can't thank you enough," Will said.

I beamed. "We're just glad we're able to help."

"Tania said the hotel has offered for us to have the ceremony and reception in their dining hall, but it won't feel the same. The café will be just great, as long as you can fit us all."

"I'm certain we can," I replied, although I wasn't certain at all. Whatever, we'd make it work.

A few moments later, Cassie hung up from Will and hugged both Paige and me. "You guys! It's perfect. Thank you."

Twenty minutes and a lot of frantic organization later, Paige, Marissa, and I clambered into an old, classic wedding car, Cassie's dress and veil draped carefully across our knees. We shook out our wet umbrellas as Cassie jumped into the front seat.

"Where to, ladies?" Josh grinned back at us from the front seat, a chauffeur's hat on top of his head.

"Where'd you get that?" Paige asked.

"It came with the car. Like it?" He waggled his eyebrows at us.

"Very appropriate," I replied.

"Okay, listen up, driver." Paige was taking control. "You need to drop Bailey and me at the Cozy Cottage first so we can get on with things, then go on to Cassie's place where she and Marissa will meet Cassie's parents."

"Yes, ma'am," Josh replied, playing along.

"And driver?"

"Ma'am?"

"Don't spare the horses." Paige put on that weird accent she'd used once before, trying to be Lady Crawley from *Downton Abbey*. It was just as terrible as it had been the first time, but no one cared. We were saving the day!

Josh's face broke into a cheeky grin. "Yes, ma'am!"

"He'll end up making some coffee-themed T-shirt about horses now, you watch," Paige said. As the owner of Ned's Coffee, Josh was famous for his corny but cute T-shirt slogans. He'd won Paige over with a T-shirt with the words "I am brew-tiful" a while back. As I said, corny but cute.

I let out a sigh. Why did there have to be so many happy couples in this city and, what was even worse, in this very car?

As we sped toward the city, Cassie called her parents, telling them what had happened and where we were now holding the wedding. Paige, Marissa, and I texted everyone we could think of on the guest list about the change of venue, hoping not to miss anyone.

Despite it being Tania the wedding planner's job, I googled a table and chair hire place, hoping to find someone who could do it with zero notice. The voice of the guy at the appropriately named Quick Hire dripped with sarcasm when he found out I needed equipment in the next hour, but he agreed to deliver what we needed in time.

I heaved a sigh of relief. Now all we needed to do was use every glass, every plate, and every utensil in the café. I tried not to think of the mountain of dishes at the end of the night.

"OMG!" Cassie's hand flew to her face. "The flowers were in the marquee."

My mind instantly darted to Addison's shop. Although we needed the space to host this wedding, it would have been very convenient if she were still here and not lounging around on a beach, all loved up with her boyfriend in Florida.

"Get Tania onto it," Paige suggested.

"Are thirteen-year-olds good at finding flowers?" Marissa asked with a scoff.

"You know what? The rest of the flowers don't matter." Cassie looked back at us from the front seat. "We've got the bouquets."

Marissa placed her hand on my forearm. "I'll text Ryan." Her voice was quiet.

My eyes darted to her face, my chest tightening at the mention of his name. In all the collapsing marquee wedding disaster excitement, I'd temporarily forgotten Ryan was one of the wedding guests.

"Sure, thanks." I gazed out the window as I chewed the inside of my lip. It was easy to avoid someone when you didn't actually have to see them. This was a whole different ball game. I knew I needed to be strong, I knew I needed to push my feelings for Ryan down, deep inside where he couldn't touch them.

Where I'd be safe.

As miserable as I was without him, I didn't know if I could do it.

By the time Josh parked the classic car outside Cassie's place the rain had abated, at least temporarily. Josh grabbed her suitcase from the trunk as Paige, Marissa, and I helped her carry her wedding dress inside, trying not to crush the delicate silk and lace.

Once in her apartment, we hung the dress up on the back of her closet door. I glanced at my watch. As much as it would be fun to stay here with the bride-to-be, we needed to leave—and *now*.

Cassie saw us to the door just as her mum arrived, balancing a box in her arms.

"Honey!" Cassie's mum, Cheryl placed the box carefully on Cassie's kitchen counter and drew her into a bear hug. "Oh, honey. Are you okay? This must be so hard for you."

"I'm fine, Mum." Cassie's calm smile surprised us all. For a woman whose wedding had changed irrevocably in the last hour, she was very chilled out. "It's actually working out pretty perfect, thanks to these two."

Cheryl took Paige's and my hands in hers. "You two are angels sent from above, do you know that?"

I blushed at the compliment. "Well, not angels, exactly. More like friends who happen to own a café." I laughed. "But thanks, Mrs. Dunhill."

"It's Cheryl, and you are angels." She shot Paige and me a knowing look. "Now, what do you need me to do, honey?" She nodded at the box. "I brought the bouquets, as you asked."

"We need to go," Paige said, glancing at me. "We've got a lot of work to do before the big moment."

"You see? Angels." Cheryl's hand was over her heart as she smiled at us both.

"Cassie? I'm sorry we can't be here for you, doing all the brides-maid-y stuff," Paige said.

"Don't be silly. You two have a much more important job to do now."

I smiled at her. "We are going to make this the wedding of the year, so don't you worry."

"And you're going to look so beautiful," Paige added.

Cassie's eyes began to well with fresh tears. "You guys! I can't cry again," she sniffed, fanning her face. "My makeup will run, and there's no Justine anymore."

"I'm on it," Marissa said. "All that paint-by-numbers I did as a kid has to translate into makeup expertise. Or at least, I hope it does. Now you two, go." She looked at Josh, who had been waiting impatiently in the wings. "You, too, Josh. Get these two super-chicks to the café so they can get on with saving the day!"

AS IF BEING bridesmaids and caterers at the same wedding wasn't enough stress in our lives, doing it all at our café, that was set up *as* a café, could have pushed us over the edge.

Lucky for us, we had a host of helpers. Josh refused to leave until he'd helped us work out our hastily drawn up floor plan, calling Nash in as some much-needed muscle. Cassie's dad, Joe, arrived ten minutes after us with her brother, Luke, and her aunt and uncle, Jim and Bev. They were all more than happy to muck in and get the place looking great. #TotalGodSends

Tania arrived and started directing people to do things before Paige and I were forced to take her aside for a moment and explain what we had planned. Frankly, she wasn't helping in the slightest, and giving her the job of pushing chairs into tables seemed like the best use of her "expertise."

"I know you probably won't believe it, but this is my first wedding planning gig," Tania said.

"Really?" Paige replied.

"I can't believe it's turned into a total catastrophe, and we need to have the ceremony *here*." She ran her eyes over our café, pulling a look of distaste. "I mean, this is a café, not a stately home, or even a marquee."

"Well, we like it here," I said, shooting Paige a look as I moved Tania out of earshot with a firm hand on the small of her back. Quick Hire had delivered the tables and chairs, and people were currently unstacking them and laying them out. "Can I leave you in charge of ensuring there's an even number of chairs at each of these tables?

"You sure can. That'll be easy for me."

"Good. I knew I could trust you with this."

With Tania no longer trying to order us around, I used the keys Addison had arranged for us to collect on our way here to open the double doors between our two shops. The florist shop was completely empty, which meant it was the perfect blank canvas for us to work with. Paige followed me through the shop and out into the courtyard, where there were still a few wrought iron tables and chairs left from when Addi had the shop.

"This place is gorgeous!" Paige took in the ivy-covered exposed brick walls and the cobbled ground. The pitched roof was made of glass, and when the sun peeked through the clouds, it streamed into the space, lending it an almost ethereal quality. Even if it was pouring outside, I knew this place would work. It would give Cassie and Will what they wanted—a romantic and whimsical setting in which to commit their lives to one another.

"It is, isn't it. There's something about this courtyard."

"I know." Paige's eyes softened as she smiled at me. "Cassie and Will are going to love it."

"Hi, ladies!"

We turned to see Sophie striding into the room, a broad grin on her face. "This is all a bit dramatic, right?"

I nodded. "Totally. We're glad you're here."

"Jason and Brett are bringing the food into the kitchen. It's just started to rain again, so it's a good job we have Brett, too."

"The cake?" Paige asked.

"Got it. It's already on the counter. You did a fantastic job, Bailey. It's beautiful."

"It wasn't all my work, Paige helped bake and prepare it." It was true I'd been the one to decorate it after watching YouTube clips on how to do it. I discovered a creative flair I didn't know I had, and it'd helped to occupy me in my post-break-up slash post-victimization malaise. "We've been 'feeding' the cake every week for a month."

"You make it sound like a caged animal." Sophie pulled a face.

"Everything's unloaded in the kitchen," a masculine voice behind me said.

I turned as Dan's doppelgänger, Jason, stepped through the arched entranceway into the courtyard. My heart leapt into my mouth as he flashed his grin at me, just the way it had every time I saw him.

I cleared my throat and looked away.

Paige stepped in. "Thanks. We're on our way out. Can you help the guys? They need some extra hands out there. Just don't let the girl who looks like she's in high school boss you around."

"I'm on it," Jason said and left.

Paige put her hand on my arm and said in a quiet voice, "You okay?"

Paige knew Jason reminded me of Dan, and she knew I found it difficult to be around him because of it. "Yeah, I'm fine. It's just a shock to see him, you know?"

"I get it. Josh told me it's coming up three years since Dan passed away."

I nodded, wringing my hands together. "Saturday's going to be a tough day."

"I know. But you know what? It's three years."

I shot her a sharp look. "What's that got to do with anything?"

She shrugged, her lips forming a thin line. "Just it's a long time ago, and I want you to be happy. You deserve to be happy."

My thoughts bolted from Dan to Ryan. My throat tightened.

And then, as if by merely thinking about him I had conjured him up. There he stood, under the archway, a box in his hands, his eyes focused on me.

Chapter 23

"HEY, RYAN," PAIGE SAID, her eyes swiveling from him to me and back again. "I'll catch up with you in a moment, okay? I've got to go . . . do . . . something."

Before I could stop her, she swished by Ryan and out of the courtyard, leaving us alone together. Rain went *pitter-patter* on the skylights above us as my heart beat hard against my ribs.

"I heard you could do with some help." Ryan's smile was tentative.

My tummy tightened at the sight of him—his handsome face, the way his bulk filled the room, his sheer masculinity.

I knew a part of me wanted him to drop that box in his hands, take me in his arms.

Never let me go.

But I couldn't let that happen. Not if I wanted to hold Dan in my heart forever, the way I knew I needed to do.

I glanced down at the box in his hands. "What's in there?" My voice had a distinctive tremor. I cleared my throat and forced a smile.

"Fairy lights. We had a bunch in the office. When Marissa told me you were having the wedding here, I thought they might work."

"Fairy lights would be . . ."

"Perfect?" His smile reached his eyes, lighting up his handsome face.

I nodded, averting my gaze. The last thing I could do was let myself get lost in those warm, hazel eyes of his. "Totally perfect. We don't have any flowers, you see. They kind of got squashed."

He raised his eyebrows. "Squashed?"

"In the marquee."

He nodded. "Right. Lucky no one was in it at the time."

"Yes." I curled my fingers at my sides. "Anyway, thanks a lot for these. Is it just one box?" My tone was purposefully brisk, efficient, as though delivering a bunch of fairy lights was the only reason he was here in the courtyard with me now.

"Nope. Got a bunch of them in the trunk of my car. I'll go bring them in."

I nodded, my lips forming a thin line. "That would be great." I took a few steps closer to him in order to walk by, my eyes trained on the old florist shop beyond.

Being this close to him, alone, was a danger I couldn't allow myself to remain in for long.

"I need to go check on the food. There's . . . there's a lot to do."

"Bailey." His voice was low, reverberating through me.

I closed my eyes and bit my lip. I didn't turn around, didn't dare chance it.

"Bailey, please look at me. I think you owe me that much. Don't you?"

I scrunched my eyes shut tight, swallowed, and turned to face him. He was right. I did owe him that—and so much more. Here he stood, helping us out when I'd ended things with him without any explanation.

He was a good man. He deserved better than I'd been able to give him.

I opened my eyes to see the box of lights at his feet, sadness written across his face.

"Amelia and I met once. That's all. She called me."

"Okay."

"She wanted me to come back to her, said she'd made a mistake."

I blinked at him. "She did?"

He nodded, biting his lip. "I turned her down."

"Wh-why?" I stuttered, not wanting to admit to myself what I wanted his answer to be.

"Because of you."

I hung my head, my heart contorting in pain. He reached out and touched my chin gently with his fingertips. I had no choice but to look up at him, my breath shortening.

His eyes bore into me. "You once told me I was worth waiting for."

I nodded, remembering how I'd uttered those words on our first date at the ball, that magical evening when everything seemed possible between us.

We were stuck in some kind of sick loop. Me wanting to be with him and him not being ready; him wanting to be with me and me not able to do so. All in all, it was a hopeless business.

Ryan and I were clearly never meant to be.

I nodded, my heart beating so hard it felt as though it had moved up into my throat.

"I just wanted you to know that *you're* worth waiting for, too."

I opened my mouth to speak, closed it again. I couldn't trust my voice, couldn't allow myself to say what I wanted to say.

I'm yours.

Instead, I shook my head, sucking in air. "No." I backed away from him, banging against the archway.

"You okay?"

"Yes, I . . . I need to get going."

"Yeah, we've got a lot to do."

"We?"

His smile was warm, heart-melting, drawing me in. "Yes, *we*."

I blinked, breaking the spell. I glanced at the box on the floor behind him. "Can you be on fairy light duty?"

"Being in charge of fairy lights sounds very manly." He chuckled, and it rumbled right through me.

I shifted my weight and rubbed the back of my neck. "I'm quite sure you'll cope." I turned and walked out of the courtyard, through the old florist shop, and back into the hubbub of the café. If there really was safety in numbers, this was where I needed to be—not alone in that magical courtyard with a man making it clear how he felt about me.

Telling me I was worth waiting for.

No. I couldn't think about that now. We had a wedding to prepare for, and less than two hours before the bride and groom were set to walk down an aisle we had yet to create.

"I'll go get the other boxes," Ryan said as he walked past me.

"Sounds great." I kept my tone light, business-like.

I surveyed the room. Our helpers had laid the tables out as we had instructed, and someone had managed to find enough white table cloths to cover each one, making the place look more like a high-end restaurant than our familiar, homely café.

"It's starting to come together, right?" Paige reached my side.

"It is. Great job, partner." I smiled at her. "What's happening with the food?"

"Sophie's got it all under control. She's amazing. We're going to have to pay her more."

"Totally. I'm going to the kitchen to check on things." I stepped into the kitchen and my eyes landed on Jason. With Ryan's declaration, I'd completely forgotten he was here.

Talk about being assaulted from all angles.

I stood in the kitchen entranceway, digging my nails into my palms. *I can't forget about Dan.* I knew I needed to focus on anything but Ryan.

Sophie walked into the kitchen behind me. "Jas? Can you help one of the guys out here?"

"Sure thing." Jason swept by me, flashing me an easy grin as he went out into the café.

"The chef's here," Sophie said.

I turned and greeted the chef and her two helpers we'd hired to do the cooking we couldn't do ourselves at the wedding. As I said, being a bridesmaid and the caterer at the same wedding certainly came with its challenges. And neither Paige nor I wanted to miss any part of this wedding if we could help it.

"You seem to have pulled things together pretty well," the chef, Leonie, said.

"We've had a lot of help."

"You need that. Right. Tell me what I need to do."

I took her through the ingredients, refreshing her on what dishes needed to be prepared and when. I had full trust Leonie and her small team could handle the task ahead. She'd worked in catering for years, only giving it up recently when her third child had come along. As she'd said to me, it turned out she loved being around her kids more than she loved being around food, but she was always in need of some extra cash.

With Leonie and her team settled in, I checked the time. We had just over an hour to go, and there was still plenty to do. I squeezed my way passed the busy kitchen staff and out into the storage area out back. The cake was sitting on one of Nona's decorative silver cake stands, looking regal amidst the café's boxes of dry ingredients and coffee beans.

I collected it up in my hands then walked through the kitchen and out into the café once more. Paige and the team had done a fantastic job. With the tables all in place, the room had completely transformed.

"Bailey, over here." Paige indicated a small table with no chairs near the counter.

With great care, I placed the cake on the table, and we both stepped back to survey it.

"Perfect," Paige said with a smile.

"It is."

"If you don't say so yourself." Paige nudged my arm with her elbow.

I laughed. After the emotional waves I'd ridden on today, it felt good.

"I think the band should play over here." Paige walked over to the other side of the counter.

"Great spot. Out of the way."

"We'll need to clear away some of the tables to dance, of course. But that's what the burly men like Josh are for." She grinned at me.

I tried not to think of another burly man, currently in charge of fairy lights.

Yup—failed.

"Have the drinks been delivered?" Paige asked.

"Yes, Sophie said they got here a while ago. Lucky for us we already have a liquor license, right?"

"Hey, you have got to see the courtyard," Tania said, sidling up to us, her eyes wide. "It's spectacular. That cute guy with the beard did a great job."

"Tania's right. Ryan weaved his magic out there, that's for sure."

I pushed my hair behind my ears. "Sure. I'll check it out. Then we need to get into our dresses. Will's going to be here soon."

Paige bit her lip, her grin wide. "I can't believe Cassie's getting married. The first of our Last First Date pact."

"True." I kept my tone light.

I didn't want to think about the Last First Date pact. Not now, not ever.

I wandered through the café to the open double doors, leading into the florist shop. I stopped when I saw the trail of fairy lights forming an aisle. They ran along the floor, leading through the old florist shop, out into the courtyard. Someone had put some black-out material up over the windows in the shop, and hung lights in a swoop from either wall, meeting in the center. It looked like the ceiling of a marquee, only in lights—and not collapsed in a soggy mess on the lawn at The Windsor Inn.

I walked between the rows of lights, my mouth dropped open. The florist shop had been transformed into something whimsical, something magical. It was bare but for the lights, enough room for many of the guests to stand and watch the ceremony.

I reached the courtyard and my hand flew to my chest. A smile crept across my face as I took it all in. With the sun now buried in layers of dark clouds, the myriad of fairy lights adorning the walls glinted and sparkled, winking at me. I looked up to a luminous stream of lights, hundreds of them, hanging from the ceiling, stopping just two or three feet above my head.

"Do you like it?"

I dragged my attention from the lights to Ryan. He was standing to the side, a hopeful look on his handsome face.

"Like it? I *love* it." My voice came out almost in a whisper.

He beamed at me. "Jason and I make a great team."

My eyes darted from Ryan to Jason, who was straightening up to look at me.

"Ryan's right. Fairy lights are *so* manly." He chucked Ryan on the arm.

My eyes slid from Jason to Ryan and back again. Their eyes were aimed at me, and as I looked back at them both, standing among the lights, I had to swallow down a lump forming in my throat.

It was like my past and my present colliding. Two men, side by side.

"I'll leave you to it," Jason said, flashing me his grin.

"Good work, man." Ryan shook his hand and slapped his back, the way men do.

"Yeah, just remember, fairy lights are packed full of testosterone." Jason beat his chest.

Ryan laughed. "Totally, dude."

Jason swept by me out of the courtyard.

"Thanks for this, Ryan. Cassie and Will are going to love it."

Ryan took a step closer to me, the fairy lights illuminating him, rendering him even more handsome than before. Not that I'd thought that was humanly possible.

"I didn't do it for them."

"But . . ."

"I did it for you, Bailey. This," he looked around the room at the twinkling lights, "is all for you."

Right on cue, my heartbeat sped up. I tried not to notice the way his proximity made my whole body tingle, the way I had to stop myself from reaching out to touch him, to feel his lips on mine once more.

"You did?" I managed.

He reached out and cupped my face in his hand, his eyes electric. "Bailey, I want you to know I'll wait for you. However long it takes."

I looked up into his eyes, my heart pounding like a drum machine. Maybe it was the romance of the setting, the lights twinkling around us, maybe it was the fact one of my best friends was about to commit her life to her man on this very spot? I didn't know.

What I did know was in that moment all I wanted to do was to kiss him.

I moved closer, sliding my hands around the back of his neck. I closed my eyes and reached up, crushing my lips to his, breathing in his scent, my body melting at his touch.

"Bailey." His voice rumbled through me.

I kissed him once more then pulled away. Although my body screamed at me to return to those lips, to feel his arms around me once more, this could only be one thing.

Goodbye.

Until my heart was free, it could never be Ryan's.

I looked down, breaking our spell. "I'm sorry," I whispered. "Don't wait for me."

"Why? Please, you've got to let me know. We might be able to fix it."

How could we fix anything?

"I . . . I just can't."

"Why? Tell me." His voice was suddenly cold, harsh, insistent.

My legs began to shake, my breathing became ragged. "I'm in love with someone else."

Ryan blinked. "But—"

I shook my head. "Don't say it."

He reached his hand out and touched my arm. "Bailey, he's gone."

I pulled away from him and clenched my jaw tight, my heart pounding. I shook my head and placed my hand over my heart. "Not in here, he's not. *Never* in here." I fought to stay calm.

He dropped his hand to his side, opening his mouth to speak.

Without waiting for a response, I turned and walked away on trembling legs.

Away from Ryan.

Back to the safety of my grief.

Chapter 24

MARISSA, PAIGE, AND I stood on the sidewalk outside the Cozy Cottage Café, holding umbrellas, waiting for Cassie to get out of the car. It was pouring down. The weather gods had made sure we knew we'd made the right decision to have the wedding here.

"Oh, Cassie. You look so beautiful." Paige had tears in her eyes as we helped Cassie straighten her dress as she stepped onto the sidewalk.

Paige was right. With her long auburn locks in soft curls around her face, her dress the perfect mix of tradition and modernity, Cassie radiated happiness and beauty. And her dress was stunning. It was inspired by the very gorgeous dress Kate Middleton wore on her wedding to her own prince. Unlike Kate's, the sleeves were capped, the bodice in a sweetheart neckline. The skirt was A-line, dropping to the ground, her veil attached to a comb adorned with fresh freesias at the back of her head.

As pretty as she looked every day of the week, Cassie looked more beautiful than I'd ever seen her right now.

"You okay, honey?" Joe, Cassie's dad said, placing his hand on her back.

"I am, thanks, Dad." She beamed at him. "I'm more than okay."

"Well, then, let's do this." He offered her his arm and she took it.

"Yeah, let's do this," Marissa echoed.

Paige, Marissa, and I, dressed in our matching bridesmaid dresses, echoing Cassie's with the sweetheart neckline and A-line skirt, got into line. We were ready to walk down the fairy light trimmed aisle.

Will and his brother, his best man, Michael, had arrived about fifteen minutes ago. Even though he'd made jokes and laughed about "Dunny" being a last-minute runaway bride, I could tell he was excited, and perhaps a little nervous, too. He was now standing at the end of the fairy light trail, waiting for his bride.

Marissa pulled the front door ajar and gave a signal to the band to start playing. As the first lines of "God Only Knows" by the Beach Boys were played, Marissa pulled the doors to the café open and stepped inside. Paige followed, and then it was my turn.

I turned and flashed a grin at Cassie whose smile shone back at me. I stepped into the café, which no longer looked like my café at all. It was packed full of smartly-dressed people, all watching us as we made our progress across the floor and down the aisle to a beaming Will.

I gave him a quick wink and took my place by the other bridesmaids. I watched with pride as Cassie and her dad walked toward us, both radiant, both grinning from ear to ear.

I glanced at Will. I've been to a few weddings in my life, and one of my favorite things to do has always been to watch the groom as he first clapped eyes on his bride, dressed in her wedding gown. Almost everyone watched the bride. Not me. I wanted to see the love in the groom's eyes.

And in Will's eyes, there was enough love to last a lifetime.

Anyone in that room could tell by the look on his face as she walked down the makeshift aisle. He adored her.

I felt a lump rise in my throat and tried to swallow it away.

Father and daughter reached the end of the aisle. Joe kissed his daughter on the cheek and took his place next to a tearful Cheryl, dabbing at her eyes with a tissue.

The music stopped, and Will took Cassie's hands in his. As the ceremony began, I looked out at the sea of people before me. I saw Josh and Nash, standing together over at the side. I saw Cassie's brother, Luke, standing with a pretty girl.

And then my eyes landed on Ryan.

Unlike everyone else in the room, he wasn't watching the bride and groom. He was watching me. I held his gaze for a beat, two, my heart giving a little squeeze.

He loves me, he's waiting for me.

If things were different . . .

But they weren't.

I tore my eyes from him, focusing instead on Cassie and Will.

As they were pronounced husband and wife to a cheer from us all, Will took Cassie's face in his hands, bent down, and they kissed. Fresh cheers erupted from the group, and the newly-weds turned and grinned.

The band began to play "What a Wonderful World" by Louis Armstrong, and Cassie and Will walked together down the aisle, grinning and saying hello to people as they went. I waited for Marissa and Paige to follow, then walked behind through the arch and the transformed florist shop and out into the café.

"Congratulations, you two!"

As we hugged and kissed the newly married couple, the atmosphere was full of hope for their future together. The guests poured through the double doors and the band moved onto their next song, a cover of an Ed Sheeran classic.

"Well, that went better than I'd expected," Tania said.

I let out a laugh. She had to be the worst wedding planner in the city. No, scratch that: the whole freaking country!

"I'm going to get a drink." Tania disappeared into the crowd.

"We've decided to have the photos in the courtyard," Cassie said. "We were meant to do them at The Windsor Inn on that little bridge they have over the stream, but that plan didn't exactly work out."

"They'll be wonderful here. Are you ready now?"

"Yup." She beamed at me. "And thank you so much for all this." She looked around the café. "Walking up that aisle with all the lights, all my friends and family looking on? Well, it was amazing. Having the wedding here is better than I could ever have dreamed."

I returned her smile. "So, you're happy?"

She glanced at Will who shot her a smile. "Oh, yes."

I took her hand in mine and gave it a squeeze. "I'm so pleased. Right, let's organize this rabble for photos."

Cassie and I rounded up the wedding party, and we all made our slow progression through the throngs of people, everyone wanting to congratulate the happy couple. I walked through the double doors into the old florist shop and waited for Cassie, Will and the rest of the wedding party to catch up.

"Hey. Bailey, right?"

I turned to look at the man at my side, my eyes almost popping out of my head when I saw who it was.

"Adam?"

He smiled at me. "Yeah, that's right. From the speed dating night."

"That's right." *Otherwise known as the night you didn't pick me.* "What are you doing here?"

"Shelley brought me. She's one of Cassie's cousins. She's my roommate, nothing more."

I wondered why he was telling me that. "Good to know."

"Look, I need to tell you something. I was a bit of a jerk that night."

"No, you weren't."

"I was. I really wanted to see you again, but I was kinda intimidated by you."

I blinked at him. "You were?"

"Well, yeah. Look at you. You're gorgeous, smart, you run your own successful business. What guy *wouldn't* be intimidated by you?"

I let out a light laugh. I could get used to being complimented by cute men. It felt nice. "I don't see it, but I'll take it all the same."

He paused, his eyes on my face. "Will you go out with me now?

It may be Dutch courage—" He raised his beer bottle. "Although I've only had a couple of sips so far, so I'm not sure I can claim it."

I smiled up at him. What would have happened if he'd written my name down the night of the speed dating—if we'd been a match? Would I have fallen for Ryan? Would I have found myself in the mess I'm now in, wrestling with my feelings for two men?

Of course, I would never know. And I wasn't going to try a re-set with Adam now.

"Are you ready?" Paige appeared at my side.

"Sure." I glanced back at Adam. "Thanks for the offer, but I think I have to pass."

He shrugged. "It was worth a shot. See you 'round." He ambled off.

"What was that about?" Paige asked as we walked side by side down the fairy-lit aisle.

"Just some speed dating closure."

She shot me a quizzical look. Before I had the chance to offer any more details, the newly-weds and the rest of the bridal party arrived, and the photographer began to direct us for a series of photographs.

Once Cassie and Will's family arrived for their session, I took the opportunity to slip out to the kitchen to check on the food. We had one-hundred-and-fifty hungry guests to feed. After the marquee disaster, this needed to run smoothly.

"Bailey? Can I talk to you?" Marissa followed me as I made my way past the cake and around the counter.

I turned and smiled at her. She couldn't warn me off dating Ryan anymore. "Sure. Follow me to the kitchen."

She nodded and did as I suggested. With the place full of busy caterers it was only marginally quieter in here, so I gestured to the back door and we slipped by the busy kitchen staff out into the alleyway behind the café.

I closed the door over. "What's up?"

Things had been a little weird between us since she'd told me about Ryan seeing Amelia. Sure, we'd hung out, and I'd even gone to a dog park with her and her cute dog last Sunday morning. But there was this unspoken feeling between us now, something I couldn't quite put my finger on.

"Look, I think I was wrong." Her features were tense.

"About . . .?"

"Ryan."

"Oh."

"He did meet up with Amelia, and I think seeing her brought up some stuff for him, but she said she wanted him back. Bailey, he turned her down."

I nodded. "I know."

Her eyebrows shot up to her hairline. "You do?"

"He told me about it before the wedding."

"And?" Her eyes were full of expectation.

I shifted my weight from foot to foot. I tried not to think of the words Ryan had said, the way he'd looked at me with such soft, loving eyes. I shook my head. "And nothing."

"Nothing?" She knitted her brows together. "But . . . but I saw how he looks at you. Him turning Amelia down is huge, don't you see?"

I nodded, drawing my lips into a thin line.

She took a step closer to me. "Bailey, you've got to know he's in love with you."

I cast my eyes down, wishing the ground would open and swallow me whole. I'd already had one difficult conversation with Marissa's brother today, now I was in another one with her *about* her brother.

She leaned back on her heels. "Are you not in love with him?"

I wrung my hands and looked up at her face, creased with concern. Immediately, I looked away, chewing the inside of my lip. I could feel her eyes on me, studying me. After a deep breath, I glanced back at her.

Her eyes were wide, her jaw dropped open. "You are in love with him. Aren't you?"

Although it was posed as one, I knew it wasn't a question.

And I also knew she was absolutely right.

As hard as I'd tried to bury my feelings for him, it was the truth, plain and simple. There was something about him, something I'd seen in him the day we'd met, when he was a shell of a man. Even then he'd drawn me in, made me want to know more about him.

And then, once we'd spent some time together, getting to know one another, having some fun together, my feelings for him had grown. Even when I got scared, knowing he'd touched my heart in a way I hadn't known since Dan, the feeling was there—this was big.

Marissa's hand flew to her mouth, her eyes almost popping out of her head. "Bailey, that's wonderful!" She collected me in a hug. "You two are such a great couple. Oh, my gosh, you're the last of the pact. It's worked. It's worked for everyone!"

Her words washed over me. I didn't want to think about Last First Dates, I didn't want to think about Ryan. "I . . . ah, I have to get back to the kitchen."

Her eyes bored into my face. "I don't get it. You love him, he loves you. What am I missing here?"

"Nothing. It's just . . . complicated, I guess."

"Complicated? But—" Her expression changed as understanding dawned. "Because of your fiancé."

My insides twisted. I wrapped my arms around myself.

"Bailey." Her face creased in concern.

I put my hands up to stop her, shaking my head vehemently. "Don't."

"I know you loved him, I know he was incredibly important to you. But he's gone."

I locked my jaw and glared at her. Two members of the Jones family had pointed that out to me in one night. *How fan-freaking-tastic*. "I know that."

She let out a puff of air. "You need to allow yourself to move on."

"You don't get it. *He* was 'the one,' *he* was my Last First Date." Hot tears threatened my eyes.

"But you agreed to the pact . . ."

"It was a mistake."

She didn't reply. She simply gaped at me.

I turned on my heel and stomped down the alleyway toward the door. I turned back to glare at her. "If you lost Nash, if you'd been dating him for years, you were engaged to marry him, would you just 'move on'?"

She opened her mouth to speak, paused, and then shook her head.

My hand on the doorknob, I paused. "Then why ask it of me?"

"Because it's been three years, right? That's a long time."

"I know that."

"And because . . . because you're in love with my brother."

I forced the door open and the music blasted out. My heart was hammering, my anger piqued.

Why did everyone expect me to just forget about Dan—forget he even existed? He was my love, my life.

Why didn't they get that?

FOR THE REST of the wedding, I buried myself completely in work, making sure everything was perfect for the happy couple. From the finger food to the dinner, I checked every detail, ensuring no one got anything less than our best.

It was so much easier than facing Marissa or Ryan—or any of them.

Paige found me in the kitchen, my Cozy Cottage apron wrapped around my waist to protect my bridesmaid's dress. I was rearranging a tray of hors d'oeuvres for Sophie, Jason, and Brett to take out to the guests. She frowned. "We've got Leonie and the staff to do this, you know."

"I know. I just wanted to make sure it was all perfect." I concentrated on my work. "You know, after the whole Fake Jamie targeting us and all? A great job is the best advertisement for our business."

I may have been speaking the truth, but our faltering catering business wasn't the reason I was in the kitchen, and Paige knew it.

"If you want to be out here, that's fine. Just make sure you sit down with us to dinner, okay? You're a bridesmaid. Cassie needs you."

I nodded at her and returned my attention to my work. "You're good to go," I said to Sophie as I handed her the tray.

"On it." Sophie flashed me a grin then left, her tray held aloft.

Thankfully, Paige followed her, leaving me to bury myself in my self-assigned kitchen duties once more.

But soon enough, the dinner preparation was complete, and I knew I had to get back out there. I couldn't let Cassie down, even though the last thing I wanted to do was to be sociable.

I hung my apron up and checked my reflection in my compact. I was definitely not looking my best. I reapplied my lipstick and fluffed up my hair, prepared as I'd ever be to face one-hundred-and-fifty people in my current state of mind.

And I got through it. I smiled at the speeches, made small talk with the other bridesmaids, drank my glass of wine, and ate the food.

And although my eyes had other ideas, I didn't once purposefully look at Ryan, sitting at a table close to ours.

By the end of the evening, I was totally wrung out from the effort of appearing normal. All I wanted was to go home, get into my pajamas, and curl up under my duvet. Hidden. Alone.

Instead, I worked into the small hours, returning everything back to where it belonged, ensuring we had a smooth transition back to business as usual on Monday morning. The hired tables and chairs needed to be stacked and returned, and I was pretty sure we'd used every utensil and plate we had in the place.

With the place empty but for Paige, Jason, and Sophie working in the kitchen, I stood on my own in the courtyard, the lights twinkling around me. I let out a heavy sigh. Despite the challenges the night had thrown at me, there was something about this place. Sure, Ryan had made it look extra special with the way he'd hung the lights, and the wedding ceremony was utterly beautiful. But there was something else about it, something that brought a sense of calm over me.

Something that made me feel I was home.

"We're all done out here." Paige was standing at the courtyard entranceway. "Did you want some help packing up the lights?"

"No, it's late. I think we can leave them for now. Addi said she still hasn't sublet the place, so there's no rush." I shrugged. "And I kinda like it like this."

Paige smiled. "It's pretty magical." She looked around the courtyard. "Cassie and Will loved their wedding here. Marquee disasters aside, I think this all worked out just great." She yawned, putting her hand over her mouth. "Well, I'm beat. I'll see you Monday." She turned and walked through the archway back into the café.

As I looked around the courtyard, a seed of an idea began to sprout and grow. A couple of butterflies tentatively batted their wings inside. I began to envisage the space around me as something else, something new. Not just an empty courtyard at the back of a florist, not just a space for my good friends to marry.

"Paige?" I called out.

She stopped, turned and looked at me. "What's up?"

I bit back a smile threatening the corners of my mouth. "I know this is usually your domain, but I think I've got an idea."

Chapter 25

AFTER DAYS OF WORKING our butts off with running the café and working on my idea Paige loved just as much as I did, Saturday the twenty-sixth came around all too quickly. And now, as I stood on the beach with Dan's family where we'd scattered his ashes three years ago, it seemed like another life.

Josh stood at my side and looked out to sea, the waves lapping gently at the shore the only sound. "Wow, it's hard to believe it's been three years, Ned. Three years since you missed that jump, since you decided to break your fall with your skull."

I smiled weakly at Josh's dark humor, my throat tight, tears threatening my eyes.

"Hey, man, did I tell you I've met a girl? Her name's Paige, and she is amazing." His face broke into a smile, his eyes lighting up. "I think you'd like her." He paused and took a breath. "Actually, bro, I know you'd like her. I . . . I wish you two could have met."

I put my hand on his arm, and he shot me a grateful look. "You're right. He would have loved Paige."

Josh turned his head. "Mum?"

Meredith stepped forward, a bouquet of flowers in one hand. She stood in silence, her head down. A seagull squawked overhead.

Eventually, she spoke. "Oh, my darling Daniel. I'm so happy we're here with you at your favorite beach. I remember how you used to run up to the waves then scream, running back to us, a huge smile on your young face. You would have only been about three or four." She pressed her lips together. "I miss you so, so much, my darling son." My heart squeezed at the crack in her voice. "There's . . ." she glanced at her husband, George, "there's nothing more to say."

Dressed in black, she looked so small, so frail. I sucked in some air, tilting my head back to stop the tears flowing.

Josh slung his arm around my shoulders, and I threw him a smile.

George, Dan's dad, took his wife in his arms to comfort her. "I miss you, too, son." His voice was strangled, sending a shiver through me.

Meredith dabbed her eyes with a lace handkerchief. "Did you want to say anything, Bailey?"

I shook my head, the lump in my throat making my ears hurt. "Maybe later."

"All right, dear." She reached out and patted me on the forearm. "Shall we release the balloons now, Josh?"

"Sure." He walked back to the tree at the edge of the beach, where he'd tied four balloons when we arrived. He untied them, returned, and handed one to each of us.

"Purple this year, huh?" I said as I took the balloon from Josh. Last year they'd been white.

"He liked purple when he was little, you know, until the boys in his class at school told him it was a girls' color. I always thought that was such a shame. But he still kept his purple dinosaur under his pillow, making sure it was hidden away when his friends came over." Meredith smiled at the memory.

"He needed to fit in," George said.

"Well, he might have wanted to conform, but he always kept his individual spark."

"That's the truth," George replied.

"I never knew that." I tried to imagine Dan as a little boy with a purple dinosaur, secretly wishing he could share it with his friends. Despite my grief, I smiled at the image.

I returned my attention to the balloon, reading the inscription: *Always loved, always remembered, forever in our hearts.*

I scrunched my eyes shut, my chest tight. Holding a balloon each, I opened my eyes and looked up at the clouds forming overhead, the patches of pale blue littered across the sky.

Josh held his balloon at my side. "I miss you, brother. Hope you're riding your bike up there, loving every minute, doing all those awesome jumps." He paused for a moment then released his balloon.

It floated up into the air, climbing away from us, until it was a small purple dot, far above our heads.

"Life has a lot less purple in it without you, Daniel. A lot less color, period. You are the first person I think of when I wake and the last person I think of when I fall to sleep. My darling Daniel." Meredith released her balloon, but I couldn't watch. My tears blurred my vision and blinking only served to spill them over until they were running down my cheeks.

Without saying a word, George released his balloon, too. He wrapped an arm around Meredith's shoulders, and they stood watching both of their balloons slip away.

I gripped onto the string of mine, my nails digging into my palms. It was as though I was holding onto Daniel, as though letting the balloon go meant letting *him* go.

And that was the last thing I wanted to do.

I sniffed and wiped my tears away with the back of my hand. I glanced at Dan's family. They were watching me, waiting for me to say my piece, to release my own balloon in honor of Dan's memory.

I froze.

"I . . . I don't think I can do it. Not this time."

"Can't do what, dear?" Meredith's voice was soft.

"I can't . . . I can't let go."

What is wrong with me?

We did this exact same thing a year ago today, and I'd managed to release the balloon then, managed to watch it float off into the sky through watery eyes. It had felt like a wonderful way to remember Dan, to do something symbolic, meaningful.

This time? I didn't know why, but it seemed different.

Final.

And it couldn't be final, not when I'd given up my new love for Dan, to keep him safe inside my heart.

I took a series of deep breaths, trying to calm myself. I willed my grip to loosen, just enough to let the balloon go, just enough so I could honor Dan the way his family had only moments ago.

I felt a warm hand on my back. "Mum? Dad? I'll see you back at the car, okay?" Josh's voice was close, his presence reassuring. "Want to sit, talk for a while?" He placed his hand over my own hand holding the string.

My panic rose. "Don't let it go. Whatever you do."

"I won't." He took the string of the balloon from me, and I rubbed my palm. "Let's go sit under that tree. It looks like it might rain."

"Sure." We walked across the grass to the grand pohutukawa tree Josh had tied the balloons to when we arrived. I stepped over the gnarly roots and found a flat spot where we both sat, Josh still holding my balloon in his hand.

He turned to face me. "This is about Ryan, isn't it?"

"What? No. It's about Dan. Me and Dan." I pulled my knees up to my chest and wrapped my arms around my legs, my eyes focused on the horizon. "It's about me not forgetting him."

"Bailey, just because you've met someone new doesn't mean you'll forget Dan."

My insides churned like a slushy machine.

"You know that, right?"

I nodded, my throat burning.

"I get it. Believe me. Falling in love with someone new must be hard. Really hard."

I snapped my head up, knitting my brows together. "Who said I'd fallen in love with him?"

He smiled at me. "You're telling me you haven't?"

My brain pole-vaulted me back to the courtyard, standing with

Ryan among the sparkling lights, his lips crushed against mine. And further back, to playing Wii Baseball with him, our games of tennis, our date to the ball.

And it was so clear, as plain as day to me.

I was in love with Ryan Jones.

"Bailey. I think . . . actually, I *know* Ned would want you to be happy. He wouldn't want you to close yourself off to love. You've gotta trust me on that."

"But—" I let out a heavy sigh. "It doesn't feel right, in here." I placed my hand over my heart. "I can't be happy, not with Dan . . . here, too."

How could I have room in my heart for Ryan and Dan at the same time?

"Bailey." I looked over into Josh's kind face, my tears blurring my vision once more. "Ned—Dan—was a great guy. You know that, and I know that. He was the best brother I could ever hope for, and I think he was a pretty good boyfriend, right?"

I gave a short, sharp nod.

"But he's gone. Not in here." He pointed to my heart. "But he's gone. You've still got your life ahead of you, Bailey. You gotta stop living in the past."

I bit my lip, trying to stem the flow of tears. I totally failed. I hung my head, allowing them to stream down my face, my shoulders heaving, my body wracked with sobs.

Josh rubbed my back. "This has been killing you, hasn't it?"

I nodded.

"Ryan seems like a good guy to me." Josh's voice was soft. "If you think you love him, then you need to follow your heart."

"But . . . Dan."

"You can still love Dan and love Ryan at the same time. It's not an either-or situation, you know?" He laughed, and I couldn't help but smile.

I took a deep, wobbly breath, gazing out at the horizon. Josh had hit the nail on the proverbial head. I'd been so worried having feelings for Ryan meant I would no longer love Dan, that I'd lost sight of the fact the human heart has an infinite capacity for love.

I let out a shaky sigh, wiping the tears from my face.

Maybe it was time to let Dan go? Maybe it was time to move on with my life, to love someone new?

But never forget. *Never forget.*

I leant over and pulled Josh in for a hug, savoring his strength, his dependability.

"Thank you," I whispered in his ear. "Thank you."

I stood up and smoothed out my skirt. Pushing himself up to stand beside me, Josh offered me the balloon. I smiled up at him as I took the string in my hand, reading the inscription once more. I stepped out from under the tree and took a deep breath, gazing up at the sky. The clouds had parted, and a patch of beautiful blue opened up directly above me.

I chose to take it as a sign.

As I let the string go, the balloon floated up and away. I repeated the inscription to myself, watching it soar above me. "Always loved, always remembered, forever in my heart."

And I knew I would always remember Dan, I'd always hold him in my heart. But, in that moment, I also knew I'd found a new love, a love for now, a love for the future.

And I needed to let him know.

Chapter 26

I STOOD ON THE sidewalk outside the Cozy Cottage and said goodbye to Meredith, George, and Josh. With his parents getting back in the car, I gave Josh an extra tight hug in thanks for his wisdom.

"Go find your happiness," he said.

I beamed back at him. "I plan on it."

"And give *my* happiness a hug. Tell her I'll see her tonight." He flashed me a grin as he got into the car.

I smiled back at him. I watched as Josh pulled away from the curb and merged with the street traffic.

I let out a long breath. I knew what I needed to do.

I had to see Ryan, and I had to see him *now*.

Only, where was he? I searched my brain. It was Saturday so he wouldn't be at work. He could be playing tennis, or just hanging out at home? Maybe out with friends?

And then I remembered. At the ball, during the awards ceremony, he'd told me today was the day they "broke ground" on his firm's new project. A new art museum with some wealthy benefactor. I remembered because it had coincided with the commemoration of Dan's passing.

And that was today.

I glanced at my watch. It was almost one p.m. He'd said we could have a late lunch afterwards, so if my calculations were correct, I didn't have a moment to lose.

I pulled out my phone and typed in "new art museum Auckland" into the search engine. Clicking on the top link, I found the address. It was on the other side of town. I chewed my lip, wondering if I could get there in time.

I had to.

I selected the app and booked an Uber. I waited, drumming my fingers impatiently on my hand.

"Bailey? I thought that was you." Paige was standing in the entrance to the Cozy Cottage, holding the door open. "How did it go today?"

I paused before I replied. "It was . . . enlightening."

She stepped toward me, allowing the door to swing closed behind her. "Enlightening? How?"

A smile teased at the corners of my mouth. "In a good way."

Paige's expression told me she was both pleased and confused. "That's great, right?"

A hybrid car pulled up quietly beside me. I glanced at the number plate—it was my Uber. I rushed over to Paige and gave her a hug. "That's from Josh."

She laughed. "Thanks, but you still haven't told me what's going on."

I dashed across the sidewalk to the car and swung the door open.

"Are you Bailey?" the driver asked.

"Sure am." I glanced back at Paige. "I will, I promise. But right now, I have to be somewhere."

She beamed back at me, clearly connecting the dots. "You go get him, girl."

The butterflies in my belly returned with reinforcements. "That's exactly what I'm planning to do."

As the car made its slow progress through Auckland's Saturday afternoon traffic, my mind was clouded with thoughts of Ryan. I thought about how he'd had to overcome his bitterness toward Amelia, how he'd shown me his vulnerability, his soft side. His willingness to work through it and give himself to me with an open heart took my breath away.

I thought about our first official date, when he made me feel like a princess in Nona's dress, when everything had seemed possible with him.

I thought of the way he'd turned up with all those fairy lights at the café, how he'd decorated the courtyard, made it into the most romantic and enchanting place for Cassie and Will to tie the knot. How he'd looked at me with soft, loving eyes—and told me it was all for me.

Most of all, I thought about how he made me feel. How he made me laugh, how his lips felt against mine, his arms pulling me into his strong body. How I'd smile, warmth spreading through my chest, whenever he crossed my mind.

As the car wound through the busy streets, inching closer and closer to my destination, I knew it could be possible to love two men at once. It could be possible to find the room in my heart, to never forget the man I'd lost, but to have a future with the man I knew I wanted more than anything to be with.

"We're here," the driver announced as he came to a stop on a street on the edge of the city.

"Thanks." I swung the door open and stepped out onto the sidewalk, an entire army of butterflies now furiously batting their wings in my belly.

I could see a cluster of people, some with cameras and lights, all standing in a circle in a large, empty lot. On unsteady feet, I walked across the uneven ground, closing in on the group. I reached the edge, scanning the crowd for Ryan.

I could hear a man addressing the crowd. "... and that is why we are so happy to be partnering together . . ."

And then I saw him.

He was dressed in a pair of navy pants and a light blue shirt, open at the neck, a white hard hat on top of his head.

He was standing next to an older man in a suit, a spade in his hand, addressing the crowd. ". . . and I all think you would agree. And now, I'd like to welcome Ryan Jones from Accent Architecture to say a few words. Ryan?"

"I'd be happy to say a few words, Rex," Ryan replied with a smile I could tell was a little hollow, not quite reaching his eyes.

I swallowed, my belly twisting in a knot. *I'm the one who stopped his smiles.*

Ryan looked from Suit Man out at the crowd, lifting his head. "Everything Rex said is true. What we're lucky enough to be doing here *is* important. We're protecting this country's art for not only ourselves, but for our children, and beyond."

I moved in a little closer to him, excusing myself so I could get a clearer view. He began to speak again. And then his eyes landed on me, a flash of recognition on his face—and something more. Something that stopped the butterflies, something that had my heart contracting in my chest. I smiled at him, my breath shortening, my heart pounding like a heavy drum.

With his eyes on me, he began to talk once more. Only this time I knew he was speaking just to me. "Because there are some things that are worth protecting, there are some things you just can't let go of. Not just for today, not just for next year, but forever." He paused, hope in his eyes, a flicker of a smile on his lips.

I returned his smile tenfold as warmth spread through my body and down my limbs. I nodded. "Yes. Yes, that's right."

The people by my side turned to look at me in surprise.

Emboldened, I continued. "Even if those things wanted to be let go. They might have changed their minds. They might have made a mistake."

I could feel more eyes on me as people stepped back to allow me to walk closer to Ryan. I took a few tentative steps and paused, wringing my hands, my eyes on Ryan.

"Did they? Make a mistake, I mean?" Ryan asked, his voice breathless.

I gave a slow nod, my breath catching in my throat. "They did."

Ryan's face lit up, and he grinned. He pulled his hard hat from his head and took a few short strides across the ground to me. With only inches separating us—and a riveted audience of about forty and a bunch of cameras trained on us to boot—I reached out to touch his hand.

"I'm so sorry, Ryan. I thought I was ready to find someone when we met. But I wasn't. I needed to let Dan go first."

"And have you? Have you let him go?"

I pressed my lips together and nodded.

His eyes flashed, his handsome face lit by the grin stretching from ear to ear. Before I knew what was happening, he leant down and picked me up off the ground, my legs draped over one of his strong arms, his other arm holding my body close to his. I slung my arms around his neck as he gazed into my eyes. "You have no idea how happy that makes me feel, De Luca."

Tears pricked my eyes. "I love you, Ryan. I love you with all my heart."

He leant down and crushed his lips against mine. And I kissed him back, my heart bursting as I breathed in his scent, safe and warm, enveloped in his strong arms.

Exactly where I wanted to be.

I was vaguely aware of applause around us as I pulled away from his lips. I glanced around and noticed everyone watching us, smiling. Cameras were trained on us, and I felt the heat of a blush creep up my cheeks.

"Do you want to get out of here?" His breath sent tingles down my neck.

"Totally."

He placed me back on my feet, taking my hand firmly in his. He turned to the crowd. "Show's over, folks." He turned to Suit Man. "This project is going to be amazing, but right now, I've got to go."

Suit Man beamed at us. "Love can do crazy things to people."

"This looks like a romantic reconciliation, am I right?" A woman with spikey pink hair thrust a microphone in my face.

I locked eyes with Ryan. "It sure is."

"What's your name, sweetie?"

The crowd parted as we walked through them and out into the lot. Ryan slipped his arm around my waist, pulling me in to him.

"I hope I didn't ruin your big moment."

"Ruin it? Are you joking? You *made* it."

We reached the entry to the lot and walked down the sidewalk, away from the prying eyes—and cameras.

Ryan stopped, turned, and looked down at me. He brushed some stray hair from my face and leant down to kiss me once more.

"God, I love you, Bailey De Luca."

"I love you, too," I whispered.

And I knew it was true, with every part of me. I could still hold Daniel in my heart, and I knew nothing would ever change that. But Ryan was here, he loved me, and I could never imagine my life without him in it again.

Epilogue

"NOW *THAT'S* WHAT I call a public display of affection." Paige giggled as she held her phone aloft for us all to see.

"Are we *still* talking about this?" Marissa folded her arms across her chest. "Who knew an architect getting the girl would be newsworthy?"

"It is because it's so romantic," Paige protested, her hand on her heart. "Bailey turning up to tell Ryan she loves him, and Ryan dropping everything to go to her? I could swoon. Seriously."

"And you're just being weird because he's your brother," Cassie added.

Marissa harrumphed. "I guess. But I am happy for you two. I just don't need it thrown in my face again and again. Know what I mean?"

I squeezed Ryan's hand, and we shared a secret look between ourselves. It had been two wonderful weeks and three incredible days since that day at the ground breaking, and I still had to pinch myself whenever I looked at him.

Ryan Jones was mine, all mine.

The story of how he had left the "ground breaking" for the new art museum to walk off with me—into a purely imaginary sunset, since it was only about one-thirty in the afternoon—had hit the local news two weeks ago. Although it was hardly headline stuff, I guess the local rag ran it because it was nice to have a feel-good story for once. A ray of light in a quagmire of terribleness.

All of us—me, Marissa, Cassie, Paige, and our respective Last First Dates—were at the Cozy Cottage Café. Well, the *new* part of the Cozy Cottage Café. You see, back when I had stood in the courtyard after Cassie and Will's wedding, I'd had an idea. An idea that had me so excited, I thought I would pop. The perfect solution for the café.

Paige had squealed with delight when I'd shared it with her, even after I suggested we back away permanently from the catering business, leaving it up to the likes of Fake Jamie and his vengeful bent to dominate all he liked.

My idea? Well, what was the thing most people thought of when they thought of the Cozy Cottage Café? That's right; cake. From Cassie's flourless raspberry chocolate cake to Paige's carrot cake with cream cheese frosting, from Marissa's orange and almond syrup cake to my *Cassata alla Siciliana*. Really, we're all about cake, people.

To distract myself from the emotional rollercoaster of my love life in the week following Cassie and Will's wedding, I'd called Addison over in Orlando to discuss my idea. She'd leaped at it, telling me the place needed to be loved and to have life breathed back into it. When I told her my plans for the courtyard, I swear I could detect an emotional quaver in her voice.

And so, Cozy Cottage High Tea was born. We specialize in cakes, with an assortment of sandwiches and pastries on the side, served with a choice of tea, coffee, or even a glass of sparkling wine.

And who better to celebrate the opening of the new branch to the café than my best friends, the women who had supported me and one another through the pact to find our Last First Dates?

And, even though we had all questioned it at some time or another, the pact had worked, for each and every one of us. Cassie had Will, recently returned from their honeymoon in Fiji, Paige had Josh, Marissa had Nash.

And me? I may be biased, but I had the best one of them all.

Ryan wrapped his strong arm around my shoulders and kissed the side of my head. "This is perfect."

I smiled up at him. "No, *you're* perfect."

His low laugh reverberated through me. "Maybe you're right, but it's only because I'm with you." His eyes teased, and my heart contracted.

I let out a contented sigh as I looked around the courtyard with its glass roof, allowing the sun to stream in. We had large plants in the corners, a hedge running around the edges. Paige and I had bought some comfortable wicker tables and chairs, we'd had cushions made of the same material as our Cozy Cottage aprons; pink with white polka dots. *So* girly. We wanted our customers to feel comfortable as they indulged in their high teas with our wide selection of delicious cakes, courtesy of Nona's recipes. Naturally.

"Bailey, this looks so wonderful." I turned to see Meredith standing in the archway, her face lit up as she smiled.

Josh bounded across the floor to greet her with a kiss. "Hey, Mum. Glad you could make it."

"I wouldn't miss this for the world." She patted his arm. "Now, Bailey, I've brought some friends with me. Do you have a table for six?"

I let out a light laugh. "Of course, we do."

"Although you'll need to book next time, Mum. Paige tells me this place is going to take off," Josh added.

"I'll be back in just a moment," Meredith said.

I glanced up at Ryan, who smiled at me, his arm dropping to his side.

"I'll come with you, Meredith. I need to go to the kitchen, anyway."

We walked through the old florist shop, which we'd furnished with more tables and comfortable seating for our high tea customers, and out into the café.

"Thank you so much for coming. And for . . . you know."

"You and that nice man, you mean? The one who looks like someone from the movies?"

I nodded. "Thor," I said with a smile.

"That's the one." She returned my smile. "Bailey, I said it before. You deserve to be happy. He seems like a good person."

My smile spread across my face as warmth spread through me, the way it always did when I thought of Ryan. "He is. He's the best."

"I'm glad. And I think Daniel would have loved what you've done with this place."

I nodded. "I think he would have, too."

Meredith gave my arm a pat before she slipped through the door to fetch her friends. I traipsed across the busy café and out into the kitchen, where Sophie was putting the final touches to three cake stands, filled with all our favorite flavors in cupcake proportions.

"They look amazing, Sophie. Thank you."

"No problem," she replied with what looked like a forced smile.

"You okay?"

"Sure."

Unconvincing.

"What's up?"

She let out a puff of air. "Don't worry about it. I'm being selfish, that's all."

My brows pinged up. "You? Sophie, you are one of the least selfish people I know. Look at how much you've done for the Cozy Cottage."

She shrugged. "I guess. It's just, well, you've all found your perfect matches. Don't get me wrong, I'm super happy for you, but I'm still languishing in terrible first date territory. I mean, I went out with a guy last week who rated me out of ten before I'd even had the first sip of my drink."

"Ouch. Can I ask what number he gave you?"

"Seven point two. Who knows how what the point two was for."

I shook my head. "I don't think you ever need to know that, honey. What you do need to know is that you'll find him, one day." My mind instantly flashed to Ryan—not only because he's my perfect match, but also because Sophie had had a crush on him. I'm sure she'd like to be in my place right about now.

"Well, if this mystical 'one day' could hurry up, that'd be nice," she said with a laugh. "I guess I've got a date on Friday with a guy I've been flirting with a little. Andrew's his name. Maybe he'll prove to be the one for me?" She nodded her head at the cakes. "Are you ready for me to take them out?"

I laughed. "I think they'll riot if you don't."

She scoops up one of the cake stands. "I'm on it. Kayla's just out back. She'll bring the pots of tea."

Kayla had worked at the café a long time ago and had recently come back, seeking forgiveness. I remembered chatting with Paige one day when Kayla had had a fit over the gluten in our food. She'd got it into her head that the gluten could seep through her skin and give her celiac disease. I know, right?

Anyway, it turned out she'd been under a lot of stress at the time with her mum getting cancer treatment and her flunking out of college. Lately, I'd become all about second chances, and Kayla re-joined our little Cozy Cottage Café family last week. Despite my nervousness, she had been amazing ever since, and we're glad to have her back.

Although, I've got to admit, I got her to help with the gluten-free options on our menu a lot more than the other staff. Just in case.

"What can I bring out?" Paige asked from the doorway.

"Here." Sophie handed her one of the cake stands.

"Hey, Bailey. Hey, Paige," Kayla chirped, her warm grin in place.

"Great to see you, Kayla. I'll help you with the tea," I said.

Sophie and Paige led the way with two of the cake stands as Kayla and I followed, balancing large pots of tea and elegant bone china cups and saucers on our trays.

As Sophie placed the tiered cake stands on the tables, all my friends exclaimed how gorgeous they looked. Marissa said she felt like the Queen of England, and Cassie grinned, going straight for her perennial favorite, the flourless raspberry chocolate cake.

Meredith and her friends arrived, and I seated them, handing them their high tea menus.

On my way to the kitchen to fill their orders, Paige followed.

"I bet Fake Jamie will be spitting tacks when he finds out what we're doing. Though I doubt high tea is his thing. Not rock and roll enough for him, I bet."

"You know what? He can try to beat us all he likes. But you and me? We're all about cake. Do you know what I say?" She shook her head. "Bring. It. On." I grinned at Paige, and she returned it tenfold.

Fake Jamie could do what he liked. I couldn't have cared any less.

Once back in the courtyard, I stood with Paige in the archway and looked around the room at the gorgeous décor, the room filled with people I knew and loved. Everyone was eating the cakes we'd made from my darling Nona's recipes. All happy and chatting with one another, the atmosphere filled with talk and laughter.

Ryan got up from one of the tables and walked over to me. He slipped his arm around my waist, and I smiled up at him.

"You've done an amazing job. You should be so proud."

"I am." I pushed myself up onto my tippy-toes and kissed his cheek. "Thank you."

"What's that for?"

"For being my Last First Date."

He raised his eyebrows, his lips curving into a smile. "Is that so?"

I nodded, never surer of anything in my life.

"Well in that case, I guess you're my Last First Date, too."

"You know you have great taste, right?"

As he smiled back at me, our eyes locked. I knew I was home—with the man I loved, in the place I loved. I may still think of Dan, and I still remember him with love. But he was now in my past where he belonged.

This. This was my present and my future.

The Last First Date pact had worked for its final member, and I was the happiest café owner in the world.

THE END

Acknowledgments

As always with a new title, I have lots of people to thank! First up has got to be my family. You are so supportive of me and my obsession with all things to do with writing. Thank you for the cups of tea, the chocolate bars, the encouragement, the patience. You rock!

Thank you to my new editor, Karan Eleni at Karan & Co. Author Solutions. Working with you has been a breeze, and your suggestions and tweaks have helped make this title what it is: something I'm very proud of.

I have much appreciation for my wonderful, super-smart beta reading team: Leanne Mackay, Julie Crengle, Kirsty McManus, Jackie Rutherford, Mary Smith, and Claire Tanton. Your advice is invaluable to me, and my books are better because of you.

Thank you to the incredibly supportive writers' groups I belong to, specifically Chick Lit Chat HQ and the Hawke's Bay chapter of the Romance Writers of New Zealand. Your support is invaluable in this wild world of writing.

To my family, as always. You are my rock and I couldn't do this without your love and positivity.

And last, but *definitely* not least, thank you to you, my readers. Without you, I wouldn't be writing, and I so love to do this! Please keep reading, and I promise to keep writing.

About the Author

Kate O'Keeffe is a *USA TODAY* bestselling and award-winning author who writes exactly what she loves to read: laugh-out-loud romantic comedies with swoon-worthy heroes and gorgeous feel-good happily ever afters. She lives and loves in beautiful Hawke's Bay, New Zealand with her family and two scruffy but loveable dogs.

When she's not penning her latest story, Kate can be found hiking up hills (slowly), traveling to different countries around the globe, and eating chocolate. A lot of it.

Made in the USA
Monee, IL
15 April 2023

31916285R00132